DAUGHTERS OF THE MOON

night
shade

LYNNE EWING

HYPERION/NEW YORK

Also in the
DAUGHTERS OF THE MOON
series:

Copyright © 2001 by Lynne Ewing

Volo and the Volo colophon are trademarks of Disney Enterprises, Inc.

First Edition
5 7 9 10 8 6 4
Printed in the United States of America

Library of Congress Cataloging-in-Publication Data
Ewing, Lynne.
Night shade / Lynne Ewing.—1st ed.
p.   cm.—(Daughters of the moon ; #3)
Summary: Jimena, who has the gift of seeing the future, must call on the skills she
developed as a gang member when Cassandra, a Follower of the evil Atrox, hatches a
plot that may destroy the moon goddesses and those they love.
ISBN 0-7868-0708-3 (trade)
[1. Supernatural—Fiction. 2. Los Angeles (Calif.)—Fiction.] I. Title.

PZ7.E965 Ni 2001
[Fic}—dc21   00-063384

Visit www.volobooks.com

For Annlee Terrell and Mollie Drake

———∽∾∽———

*With many thanks to Victor Carrillo, Jr., and
Julie Morales for sharing their lives with me,
and, of course, a special thank-you to my
wonderful editor, Alessandra Balzer*

Diana was the goddess of the hunt and of all new-born creatures. Women prayed to her for happiness in marriage and childbirth, but her strength was so great that even the warlike Amazons worshipped her.

No man was worthy of her love, until powerful Orion won her affection. She was about to marry him, but her twin brother, Apollo, was angered that she had fallen in love. One day, Apollo saw Orion in the sea with only his head above the water. Apollo tricked Diana by challenging her to hit the mark bobbing in the distant sea. Diana shot her arrow with deadly aim. Later, the waves rolled dead Orion to shore.

Lamenting her fatal blunder, Diana placed

Orion in the starry sky. Every night, she would lift her torch in the dark to see her beloved. Her light gave comfort to all, and soon she became known as a goddess of the moon.

It was whispered that if a girl-child was born in the wilderness, delivered by the great goddess Diana, she would be known for her fierce protection of the innocent.

▼

CHAPTER ONE

JIMENA CASTILLO WALKED down the rain-drenched street as if she owned the night. And she did. This was her neighborhood, the Pico-Union District of Los Angeles. She passed Langer's Deli, held her face up to the cool rain, and crossed Alvarado Street against a red light.

A Ford Torino jerked to a stop, inches from her knees. Before the driver could honk, Jimena tapped the hood of the car. The man glanced up and her eyes warned him, *You're out of your neighborhood.*

He understood and settled back patiently as

if it were normal to stop at a green light in Los Angeles. Once Jimena had crossed the street, the car screeched away.

Jimena headed toward MacArthur Park. She was tired and coming down fast. The *tecatos* peeking from their makeshift tents might think she was on drugs. If they only knew what she had really done that night, what would they think? She wondered if her true identity would frighten them or make them ask her for help. She laughed, her voice as light as raindrops.

Jimena saw a movement from under one of the benches. Pieces of cardboard slipped off a sleeping body. She felt a sudden need to stop and confess. To sit on the bench above the poor homeless person and tell him everything. She didn't give in to the urge but hurried to the path around the lake. Rain made the wet asphalt look as slick as sealskin. The giant water fountain in the middle of the lake continued to spew water into the air as if it were working hard to send back the rain.

When she approached Wilshire Boulevard, her eyes automatically scoped out the street.

Traffic was light but the dangers were big. Wilshire was the boundary of her neighborhood. She had to cross enemy land to get to her grandmother's apartment.

At the corner near the bus stop, a *klika* of enemy homegirls waited impatiently in the shadows. They looked as if they had plans to throw down some old lady when she got off the bus. Maybe someone who cleaned the floors at Cedars-Sinai Hospital or worked the tables in a West Los Angeles restaurant.

Jimena didn't slow her pace. She walked steadily toward them, head high.

The girls glanced once, twice, then with slow casual steps they ambled away from the bus bench as if they hadn't seen her.

Jimena sensed their fear. That brought a smile to her face. Her reputation was still so big that even tough *enemigas* wouldn't face her down.

She strutted past them, her heels snapping loudly on the sidewalk. She enjoyed the feel of their admiring eyes, their sideways glances and the wonder she saw on their faces. Jimena wasn't choloed out in khakis, a tight T, and long, boyfriend-borrowed Pendletons. She wore a slinky dress and ankle-breaking high heels. The rain made the dress cling to her body, so they knew she wasn't strapping. No gun. Still, they were afraid to confront her.

This time she stopped for the red light, pausing to let the *chicas* know she didn't fear them. It felt good to be the toughest *chola en el condado de Los Angeles.* She was still down for Ninth Street, her old gang, but at age fifteen, already a *veterana.* A *leyenda,* her homegirls told her with pride. Jimena had been a real badass before she understood her destiny. She glanced at the scars and tattoos on her hand. What would the *klika*-girls do if they knew her true identity?

She turned back to toss them a grin, but they were already hurrying away down the boulevard.

The light turned green. Jimena started across the street as slow, lazy thunder rolled across the night and vibrated through the ground. She eagerly looked at the midnight sky. Thunderstorms were rare in Los Angeles, and she wanted to see a jagged flash of lightning. Another thunderclap rocked the air but again without a heralding bolt of light. The rain was heavier now and cold. Jimena walked faster.

A car splashed by, its tires humming on the wet street.

"Jaguar." The word came over the rain as soft as a secret.

She stopped and looked behind her. Only Veto had called her "Jaguar," and he had been dead a year now, killed in enemy land. Could it have been those homegirls? Had they somehow gathered their courage and decided to face her? She studied the rain-drenched shadows. The glossy shimmer of wet leaves reflected the pink-and-blue neon lights. But her mind wasn't on finding enemy homegirls. She thought about Veto. The ache of missing him surprised her. How could she miss him so much after a year? She yearned for the sweet kind of love she had known with him.

She had transferred to La Brea High School

less than six months ago, and the guys there never did more than smile or ask her to dance. She could feel them looking at her when she walked down the hallways, but when she caught their glances, they looked away. Perhaps they saw the gangster in her eyes or in the curl of her lips. Veto had said she was like a jaguar; her show of teeth was a warning, not a smile. She was probably scaring the guys away without even knowing it.

She walked slower now, ears sensitive to the slightest sound. Raindrops hit leaves, grass, and car roofs, but it was one voice she longed to hear. Memories of Veto echoed cruelly through her mind. She never understood why he had gone off to enemy territory the night he was killed. She felt bitter about his death. He'd been acting crazy, but going over to enemy land without his homeboys was even too *loco* for him. What had made him go?

"Jaguar."

She heard the word clearly this time, and turned. A lean muscular young man stood silhouetted in front of a security light. He started walking slowly toward her. A gust of wind blew his raincoat open and it flapped behind him like giant black wings.

When he stepped into the amber light of the street lamp, she gasped. "Veto?"

Veto stood in front of her, his face as bold and beautiful as his Mayan ancestors', with dark flashing eyes and high cheekbones. His blue-black hair was dripping rain as if he had been following her unseen for a long time.

Her heart pounded wildly. "Veto." She spoke his name slowly this time, enjoying the luxurious feel of it on her tongue and wondered if she were dreaming. She had dreamed about him so many times since his death, and sometimes even awoke thinking he had called her name.

He stepped closer to her. There was something different about the way he looked. Veto, but not Veto. His hair was longer than he had worn it before, his skin was paler, and he had lost weight. She studied his black eyes. They blinked as if the dim streetlights were too bright.

Even as part of her recoiled, her hand reached out to touch the tiny scar on his right cheek. His skin felt warm under the raindrops. Veto, alive? Her mind rushed to find an explanation. His casket had been closed at the funeral. She had never actually seen him dead. Could the police department and the coroner's office have made a mistake? Maybe some other homeboy had been buried in his place. She weighed the possibilities. Perhaps Veto had been put in the witness protection program. That would explain his crazy behavior, if he was intending to turn *rata*. And after his funeral his mother and three younger brothers had moved back to Mexico.

"What are you doing here? Were you in the witness protection program?" she asked, hating the air that separated them.

"No, Jaguar, I'm no rat-head." He tried to smile the way he had always smiled at her, but his lips seemed stiff and unused to it. Sudden sadness burdened her heart. Had Veto been someplace where smiles were dangerous signs of weakness?

"Then what?" She couldn't say more. Her bottom lip started quivering and the tears she had been unable to cry at his funeral a year ago rolled down her cheeks.

"*Estás llorando?*" Veto clasped his arms around her. His warmth seeped into her cold skin. "I never saw you cry before."

"It's rain," she lied, even now having to be the tougher one.

He kissed the tears.

She pulled back. "Where have you been?" The words came out with hoarse anger from missing him so much.

"Lost."

"Lost? What kind of answer is that?"

"I got back to you. That's all that matters. I always told you nothing was ever going to separate us."

"So you did make a deal with the cops? Who'd you rat out?"

He turned away, and then she knew. He had too much *cora* to rat out any of his homeboys. It had to be the guy who had been selling drugs to Veto's homeboys. Only Veto was strong enough to do that. That meant he'd gone up against someone big and needed to hide.

She nodded, understanding. "You're here now. Where are you staying?"

He didn't answer her.

"Are you hanging out with your homeboys?" He was probably living from one couch to the next. That troubled her. Why hadn't anyone told her Veto was back?

He started to say something, but thunder shattered the night and Veto jerked around. When he looked back at her, stark terror covered his face.

"I gotta go." His words came out with a nervousness she had never heard in his voice before.

"Don't," she said. "Come home with me."

But already he was pulling away from her. "No, I can't. I gotta be somewhere."

"Where?" She hated the look she saw on his face. Veto has never been afraid of anything. What could be so bad that it could scare him?

Another clash of thunder shook through the ground. The alarm in Veto's face made her heart race. "What is it? What do you see?" she asked.

"Nothing." His eyes betrayed the lie.

"Tell me," she whispered. "I got your back."

Veto started to run.

"Wait," she demanded.

He turned and ran backward, smiling at her. "I'll see you soon," he shouted through the rain. "When it's safe."

"Safe from what?" she yelled.

Then her legs acted on their own and she ran after him.

New thunder shuddered through the ground. Veto turned and sprinted down the sidewalk toward the park.

"What is it?" She splashed through puddles, calling after him, "What's wrong?"

He dodged the traffic on Wilshire. She had just started after him when a truck blew its horn. She jumped back on the curb. The giant tires sprayed her with water. After the truck had passed, she could no longer see Veto.

She crossed the street and circled the park, then stood alone in the storm until her body shivered with cold and her hair was pasted against her head.

Finally she turned and walked slowly back to her grandmother's apartment building.

There was so much she wanted to tell Veto. She glanced down at the triangle of three dots tattooed on the fleshy web between her index finger and thumb. The day she got jumped into Ninth Street, Veto had tattooed the dots into her skin using ink and a pin. Later, he had tattooed the teardrop under her right eye when she got out of Youth Authority Camp. The second teardrop was for her second stay in Youth Authority. She would have gone back a third time for firing a gun, if a lenient judge hadn't sentenced her to do community service work instead. She had fired the gun in frustration when she couldn't stop her homegirls from doing a throw-down. The cops had caught her, but she wouldn't turn *rata*. She was willing to go back to camp to protect her homegirls. That was the code. But the judge had seen something different in her eyes this time and let her off with community service.

Jimena had known about her destiny by then, and she had changed. It amazed her even now, if she thought about it. Who would have thought she was meant for something so important?

She looked back at the rain-soaked shadows. What would Veto do if he did know the truth about her? He was the one who had always said there was magic inside her. *Bruja*, he had teased. He had called her a witch because she could see the future.

Secretly, she had been afraid when Veto called her gift witchcraft, because she didn't think she was seeing the future. She thought she was making the dark things happen. The first time she had a premonition, she had only been seven years old. She had been outside playing with her best friend Miranda when a picture of Miranda in a white casket crossed her mind. Then Miranda had touched her, asking her what was the matter, and another picture had played behind her eyes. She saw Miranda walking down Ladera Street as a car sped by. Shots blasted from the car window and Miranda fell to the ground, dead.

The premonition had terrified her. She had tried to keep it from coming true and made

Miranda go a block out of her way each day when they walked home from school. But then one day Jimena had come down with the flu and had to stay home. That afternoon, she heard the gunshots, and she knew.

Jimena was scared that she had caused Miranda's death. After all, she had seen it happen. Sometimes even now it bothered her that she could see the future, especially because she had never been able to stop any of her premonitions from coming true, no matter how bad they were.

She stepped across the street and headed toward one of the brick hotels that lined this part of Wilshire Boulevard. The hotels had been converted into apartment homes for poor people, but the whirling pink-and-blue neon lights with the old hotel names still lit the night sky.

Maggie Craven loved the old neon lighting and had told Jimena stories about going to elegant parties in the hotel ballrooms. Jimena imagined Maggie dancing with some movie star. She loved Maggie as much as she could love anyone, even her grandmother. Maggie had been the first person to explain to her that she had a gift that allowed her to see things that were going to happen in the future. She wasn't a witch who made the bad things happen.

Now, Jimena didn't know what she would do without Maggie. But in the beginning it had taken her almost a year to believe what Maggie had told her about her destiny. Maggie had first appeared in her dreams, urging Jimena to come see her. When Jimena had finally gone to Maggie's apartment, she had been shocked to discover the woman in her dreams actually existed. Maybe that would have been enough to convince others that what Maggie said was true, but to Jimena, Maggie's words sounded like madness.

"Tu es dea, filia lunae," Maggie told her in Latin at their first meeting. "You are a goddess, a Daughter of the Moon."

Maggie had explained that in ancient times when Pandora's box was opened, the last thing to leave the box was hope. Only Selene, the goddess of the moon, had seen the demonic creature lurking nearby, sent by the Atrox to devour hope.

Selene took pity on humankind and gave her daughters, like guardian angels, to perpetuate hope. Jimena was one of those daughters.

Jimena had been stunned. Goddess? Did such beings exist?

Maggie also told her about the Atrox, the primal source of evil. The Atrox and its Followers had sworn to destroy the Daughters of the Moon.

"Me?" Jimena had responded.

"Yes." Maggie had explained that once the Daughters were gone, the Atrox could bring about the ruin of humankind.

The words still overwhelmed her. How many people even believed in the mythical world? She'd heard the *viejecitas* tell stories of other gods who lived in the jungles of Mexico and Guatemala. The old women swore the voices of those gods could still be heard in the ruins at Tikal and Chichén Itzá. But she'd never taken their stories seriously. She didn't think goddesses really existed and if they did they wouldn't look like a *chola* with two teardrops tattooed under her right eye.

Maggie had hugged her dearly when she expressed her doubts and told Jimena that a goddess of the moon had given her many gifts and that someday she would know the truth.

Jimena wished Veto had stayed long enough so she could tell him about her destiny. He had always seen her as someone special. Her gift never frightened him the way it had scared others. Thinking about Veto now made her mind turn back to what had happened tonight. Why had he seemed so terrified? Then an uninvited thought pushed forward. Suddenly she knew his appearance had only been an illusion. Perhaps the intensity of her memory of him tonight had made her imagine him so vividly.

She turned down the walk that led up to her grandmother's apartment building. Cement lions sat on either side of the porch steps, dripping rain. As she slipped the key into the lock a sudden dread filled her. Maybe she was sensing something about the future. Something so terrible that the only way she could deal with it was to project the fear onto Veto's ghost.

She unlocked the door to the apartment building and hurried inside. The enormous stairs of the old hotel led up to a gloomy ballroom, now used only occasionally for community meetings. Framed photographs and yellowed newspaper clippings in the entrance behind dusty glass told of the days when the hotel had been what Maggie called a swanky place.

Jimena turned back and stared out the side window. An ominous change had come over the night. She shuddered, but it was more a deep inner chill that caused the cold now. She knew trouble was coming.

▼

CHAPTER TWO

JIMENA UNLOCKED THE door to her grandmother's small apartment. The air was warm with
the spicy smells of baking *chiles*. She walked
through the dark living room to the light in the
kitchen. Her grandmother stood over the stove,
making tortillas from chunks of cornmeal dough
by slapping them back and forth between her
hands and cooking them in a cast-iron skillet. A
stack of warm tortillas sat on the counter near a
line of casserole dishes.

Jimena's *abuelita* looked up. Her regal face
started to smile, but the smile was lost in a look

of astonishment. She dropped a half-formed tortilla on the counter. *"¡Parece que hubieras visto un fantasma!"*

"I did see a ghost," Jimena spoke softly. "I saw Veto."

Jimena fell into her grandmother's comforting arms. The old woman held her for a long time, and when she pulled away, her black eyes seemed anxious, as if there was something important she wanted to say. She wiped her hands absently with a towel and stared at the rain beating on the window over the sink.

"What?" Jimena asked and gently turned her grandmother back to face her.

"Cuando te caíste del cielo . . ." Her grandmother started, but then a look of astonishment crossed her wrinkled face.

"What?" she asked.

"Your moon amulet," she said, reaching for it. "It's shining." Her grandmother touched the face of the moon, then jerked her fingers back as if she had been shocked.

Jimena looked down at the amulet hanging

around her neck. It was glowing. Had the amulet been glowing before when she was with Veto? Could she have been too anxious to notice the electrical thrum her amulet made to warn her in times of danger? Maybe the apparition really had been Veto's ghost.

Her grandmother looked across the room at the small cross hanging on the eastern wall next to the picture of the Virgin of Guadalupe. "The night you were born . . ." Again her voice drifted away as if she couldn't find the right words to complete her sentence.

"The night I was born? *¿Qué?*" Jimena asked. Always when her grandmother started to tell her about the night she was born, she stopped before telling her the whole story. "Does it have something to do with what happened tonight, with seeing Veto? Tell me!"

Her grandmother opened a drawer in the cupboards, pulled out a book of matches, and walked over to the tiny table covered with flowers, candles, and the icons of saints. Her hands trembled as she lit the candle for *La Morena*. She crossed herself and was silent a moment, as if she were praying to the beautiful Madonna of the Americas to give her guidance.

Finally she came back to the table and sat down. She motioned for Jimena to take the chair across from her.

Jimena did so. She felt tense with apprehension about what her grandmother was going to say.

"Maybe seeing Veto has something to do with that night," her grandmother finally confessed. Her tiny black eyes stared at Jimena. "It never surprised me that you can see into the future, because something very strange happened the night you were born."

"Tell me." Jimena moved the casserole dishes aside so that she could lean closer to her grandmother.

"I never told anyone before, because I was too afraid no one would believe me."

Jimena's heart raced. What was the secret that her grandmother had kept all these years? She laid her hand on top of her grandmother's cold fingers.

"Your mother and I were crossing the high desert, coming into California from Mexico so you could be born in *Los Estados Unidos.* We had to hide from *la migra* and when we did, your mother went into labor early, miles from any doctor. I was sure I was going to lose you and your mother. *Venías de nalgas,* a difficult birth, and then . . ."

Her grandmother paused and looked back at the picture of *La Morena.* The candlelight flickered across the face of the Madonna, and seeing her tranquil face seemed to give her grandmother courage.

When she continued, she spoke in a voice so low, Jimena had to pull her chair closer to hear.

"A beautiful woman, like *una diosa,* came from nowhere. I thought she was a saint who had come to take you and your mother back to heaven, but then I knew she was going to help us. She didn't open her mouth, but in my mind I knew what she was saying. I could feel her words as if she were speaking. *Un milagro.* It was a miracle. She gave you the moon amulet that you always wear."

Jimena looked down at the silver amulet hanging around her neck and studied the face of the moon etched in the metal. It seemed to sparkle back the kitchen light in a rainbow of shimmering colors. Her best friends Serena, Catty, and Vanessa each had one. Jimena never took hers off.

"*La diosa* said that as long as you wear the amulet, you'll be protected." Her grandmother touched the face of the moon lightly with her crooked index finger.

Jimena clasped the amulet and wondered what would happen if she ever took it off.

"So when you were a *niña* and you told me you feared for your best friend Miranda, I warned Miranda's mother to be careful. I knew you had gifts. I knew you were different from other children."

"*Abuelita*," Jimena started. Did she dare tell her the truth? What would her grandmother do if she knew who Jimena really was?

"So maybe seeing Veto is part of your gift. Maybe you can contact the departed. *Los difuntos.*"

She stared at her grandmother. It was easy for her grandmother to believe that the dead were always around us. Each year during *Los Días de los Muertos,* her grandmother made an *ofrenda* for her grandfather, piling it high with marigolds and her grandfather's favorite foods.

But, Jimena wondered, if seeing the spirits of *los difuntos* was part of her gift, then why had she never seen her grandfather's ghost? She loved him as much as Veto.

She looked back at her grandmother. "Do you know who the woman was? *La Diosa?* Did she tell you her name?"

"Yes." Her grandmother nodded. "Diana. I asked her her name and in my mind I knew they called her Diana. I told your mother we must name you Diana, but she insisted we name you Jimena, after me."

Jimena smiled back at her. "I'm glad she did."

After a moment her grandmother continued, "So don't be worried that you saw Veto. It's all part of who you are. If we still lived in Mexico you'd be a strong *curandera* healing people."

"Or a *bruja*." Jimena laughed.

"*Una bruja nunca.*" Her grandmother shook her head. "No, your gift is for good. I know this *con todo mi corazón.*" She placed her hand over her heart.

Jimena wanted to tell her grandmother everything then, to let her know that she was fighting an ancient evil. Her heart beat rapidly, and she started to open her mouth to speak, but before she could, her grandmother spoke. "There, I've said too much already. I sound like one of those old women rambling at the bus stop to anyone who will listen."

Her grandmother glanced at the clock and the moment was lost. "Tomorrow the *señoras* from the nice suburbs will come on their way home from church and buy the *moles* to serve for Sunday dinner. I still have too much to do."

"I'll help you," Jimena offered.

"You take a warm shower and put on dry clothes first. I should have made you change your clothes before I spoke but . . ." She shrugged and changed the subject. "It's easier when your brother is here." Sometimes Jimena's brother delivered the food and collected the money, but now he was in San Diego helping their uncle open a restaurant.

Jimena nodded. It was easier for her, too, when her brother was home, because he let her drive his car even though she didn't have a driver's license yet. She'd learned how to drive when she was twelve so she could jack cars. It surprised her even now when she thought about the risks she used to take back in her old life. She felt guilty, knowing how much the arrests had hurt her grandmother.

Her grandmother bent over and opened the oven, then took a pot holder and pulled out a tray of black and blistered chiles. She removed the tray from the oven and shook the chiles into a paper bag to steam. She handed a pair of yellow rubber gloves to Jimena. "Hurry. Take your shower, then come back and peel the chiles for me, *m'ija*."

Jimena stood.

Her grandmother winked, picked up a chunk of masa and began slapping it back and forth.

"This is the last night of doing this."

Jimena nodded. Her grandmother was going down to San Diego to help with the restaurant.

Her hands stopped. "Only if you'll be all right alone. I'll stay if you need me."

"Go," Jimena answered.

"Maybe Tuesday then."

Jimena nodded.

"Now take a shower," her grandmother ordered.

Jimena hurried down to the bathroom. She bathed, put on a T-shirt and sweatpants, then came back, slipped on the rubber gloves, and sat at the table. She worked to remove the skin, ribs, seeds, and core from the chiles as her grandmother made the tortillas.

The smells of the *moles* bubbling on the stove and the rhythm of her grandmother's slapping relaxed her. Veto drifted back into memory and the ache and longing of missing him took its place in her heart.

▼

CHAPTER THREE

J

IMENA WAITED AT a bus stop on Melrose Avenue. The late-afternoon crowd pushed around her, sipping lattes and bottled water. Kids stopped to gaze at the punk paraphernalia in the shop behind her. Others tried on the trendy sunglasses that a street vendor was selling from a blanket stretched across the sidewalk.

When she saw Serena walking toward her, swinging her cello case, Jimena waved. Serena was wearing red cowboy boots and a lacy yellow sundress.

Jimena had admired Serena since the first

day Maggie had introduced them almost a year back. She would never have admitted it then because she had still been kicking it with her homegirls and putting on the *máscara* of a tough gangster. She had laughed when Maggie had told them they would be battling Followers together. There was no chance Jimena was going to let a wimp like Serena watch her back; that was one sure way to get killed. But Jimena had quickly changed her mind the first time they fought a group of Followers. Serena never backed down. Now Jimena trusted Serena with her life.

Serena sat on the bus bench, and brushed her dark hair away from her face. Her nose ring glistened in the late afternoon sun.

"So what are you *haciendo*-ing this afternoon?" Jimena asked.

"Music lesson." Serena carefully fit her cello case between her legs. "You hear the earthquakes Saturday night?"

Jimena nodded. "All that rumbling sounded like thunder to me."

"Me, too." Serena pulled the cello case closer

as an old woman sat down beside her. "The newspapers are calling it quake thunder."

"Could be. I didn't see any lightning." Jimena thought a moment. "But I can't believe those rumblings actually came from the ground and not the sky."

"The seismologists at Caltech are scaring everyone the way they're calling it an earthquake swarm. They're saying it could be a prelude to the big one." Serena pulled her student bus pass from her messenger bag.

Jimena nodded. "I don't want to be around when the San Andreas fault breaks."

An old woman sitting beside Serena leaned into them. "Earthquake weather," she whispered. "Look at the sky."

Jimena looked up at the gray cast and shook her head. "Those are just rain clouds."

Serena looked at the fast-moving clouds. "What's earthquake weather?"

"Just superstition," Jimena answered. "The old ladies where I live say they can tell when there's going to be a big earthquake because days before the sky turns gray and the air feels still and heavy on your skin."

"It's earthquake weather," the woman insisted with a crooked smile.

Jimena continued, "But the same *viejas* say you can't have an earthquake when it's raining and it was definitely raining Saturday night."

A bus pulled up to the curb and the woman hobbled onboard.

"Where were you yesterday, anyway?" Serena changed the subject. "I tried to call you to make sure you got home okay but no one answered the phone." Serena didn't need to say she had been worried. Jimena could see it from the look in her eyes. Serena glanced around to make sure no one was listening. "I thought maybe the Followers had caught up to you."

They had gone over to Hollywood Saturday night and run into Cassandra and a pack of Hollywood Followers.

Serena continued. "Then you weren't at school."

"I was at school. I just got there late. I had to

help my grandmother with the food on Sunday and then I had things I had to do the rest of the day." How could she tell Serena that she had spent Sunday looking for a dead person? She had gone to all the places where she and Veto had hung out, hoping his ghost might reappear to her. She shrugged. "And this morning, I overslept."

"What is it you're *not* saying?" Serena asked with a sly smile.

That was Serena's gift. She could read minds. Like Jimena, she hadn't understood her power when she was little. She only knew then that she was different. Sometimes in the excitement of playing, she'd forget her friends weren't speaking and she'd answer their thoughts. Even now, if she became too happy or excited, she'd answer people's thoughts as if they were saying them out loud.

"Tell me," Serena coaxed. "I know something else is on your mind."

Jimena needed to talk to Serena about Veto, but embarrassment made her hesitate.

"What?" Serena urged.

"Saturday night, I . . ." But as she started to tell Serena about seeing Veto, her amulet resonated against her chest with an electrical hum.

They both looked up, alert to danger.

Cassandra was shoving through the crowd, walking toward them. She wore stretchy black capris with a low-cut, black tank top and too much silver jewelry. Thin white scars formed a crooked S T A on her chest. She had been wildly in love with Stanton, the leader of the Hollywood Followers, and tried to cut his name into her skin with a razor blade before Stanton had stopped her. She might have been beautiful once, but evil had made her features harsh and pinched. She stopped in front of Tattoo You, a small store-front shop where kids got piercings and tattoos.

"What does she want now?" Jimena wondered.

"I told you she's been following us," Serena sighed.

"Why's she so desperate to get into a *pleito* with us?"

"Followers always want to get in our faces."

Serena tried to make light of Cassandra's sudden appearance but Jimena knew her well enough to know it troubled her.

"You'll lose," Cassandra whispered—or had she let the words slip across their minds? She was too far away for them to have been able to hear her. Jimena shuddered. She hated the way Cassandra had so easily entered their minds. She glanced at Serena, who seemed more than irritated.

"Steady," Jimena warned. "Don't do anything yet."

Cassandra had been accepted by the Atrox and apprenticed to Stanton to learn how to perfect her evil. Already she could read minds, manipulate people's thoughts, and even imprison others in her memories, but, unlike Stanton, she didn't have immortality.

"What's she up to?" Serena was upset.

Jimena shrugged. "You'd think I'd have had a premonition." She was almost always forewarned if they were going to have a serious run-in with the Followers.

"You know how she felt about Stanton," Serena said. "Maybe she suspects that I'm seeing him."

"You shouldn't be," Jimena scolded, as she had a dozen times before. "It's forbidden. If the Atrox finds out, it'll send Regulators to terminate Stanton."

"Like I don't know that?" Serena didn't take her eyes off Cassandra.

"Is he worth it?" Jimena felt apprehensive. If Regulators were powerful enough to destroy an immortal like Stanton, then Serena didn't have a chance against them. What if they caught Stanton while Serena was with him? "You're risking your life—and besides, it doesn't feel right keeping secrets from Vanessa and Catty."

It was more than that. She didn't know how Serena could trust Stanton so completely. Once Stanton had trapped Vanessa in his childhood memories. While she was there, Vanessa had tried to save a younger Stanton from the Atrox. After that act of kindness he could never harm Vanessa, but Serena didn't have the same guarantee. There was too much competition among Followers for a place of power in the Atrox hierarchy. Stanton could be using Serena. After all, the biggest prize for any Follower was the seduction of a Daughter of the Moon or the theft of her special power. The Atrox awarded such a deed by allowing those Followers into its Inner Circle.

But Serena cared for Stanton. Sometimes she actually felt sorry for him. His father had been a great prince of Western Europe during the thirteenth century and had raised an army to go on a crusade against the Atrox. But the Atrox had kidnapped Stanton to stop his father.

Serena nudged her. "Now look who's here."

Karyl left Tattoo You and joined Cassandra. He turned and smiled at them. He reminded Jimena of a lizard, the way his beady eyes darted up and down her body with frank sexual interest. That wasn't the only thing creepy about him. He looked their age, but there was something about him that seemed old and made her think he had been alive for hundreds of years.

Jimena turned slightly so that she could

watch Karyl more closely. "It's creepy the way he's just smiling at us."

"Hideous," Serena agreed. "It's as if he and Cassandra have something big planned."

"I know, but what?" Jimena knew Karyl's power. She had faced him in battle the night Karyl and Cassandra had tried to destroy Catty and Vanessa.

"They're acting weird," Serena said.

Cassandra had always been vindictive, but something was different about the way she strutted toward them now. Maybe she did know about Stanton and Serena. She stopped a few steps from them.

"Enjoy the nice weather while you can," Cassandra warned. "You won't be seeing many more days."

Behind her Karyl laughed. He opened the door to Tattoo You and Morgan stepped out and joined him. She wore a skimpy black dress and shiny black boots. A new gold hoop pierced the flesh above her eye. The skin looked bright red and sore. Jimena wondered what Morgan's parents would do when they found out what had happened to her. They'd never fully understand, but they'd see the change. Jimena didn't feel guilty about it the way Vanessa did. Serena and Jimena had risked exposing themselves in order to protect Morgan, but in the end the Followers had claimed her.

"Nice pierce," Jimena said. "You just get it?"

Morgan gave her a quick angry look and touched the gold hoop. It was something she never would have done before.

"Can you even believe that?" Serena spoke in a low snickering voice.

"Don't laugh." Jimena nudged her.

"I can't help it." Serena clapped her hand over her lips.

Jimena shook her head. She wasn't sure what she saw in Morgan's eyes now. Sorrow? Remorse? Rage? Morgan had always had an attitude that had made it impossible to be her friend, but now that she had become an Initiate she was even more edgy. Initiates wanted to prove themselves worthy of becoming a Follower. Morgan had a trace of hardness in her face now in spite of her perfect angelic features.

Cassandra's head whipped around, and she took a step backward.

"What now?" Serena asked.

"It's Catty and Vanessa," Jimena answered.

"Maybe she feels outnumbered," Serena suggested.

Jimena sighed with relief. "Good, I feel low on energy today."

Catty and Vanessa joined them on the bus bench. Vanessa had gorgeous tanned skin, large blue eyes, and shiny blond hair. She was wearing a pink slip dress and beaded slides. Michael Saratoga's jacket hung on her shoulders.

Catty was forever getting Vanessa into trouble, but they remained best friends.

"What's up?" Vanessa looked nervously down the street at Cassandra.

"Looks like the usual." Catty tried to say the words in an easy manner, but Jimena saw the way she had shuddered when she had first observed Cassandra, Karyl, and Morgan.

Catty took off her yellow slicker and leaned against the bus bench. She was stylish in an artsy sort of way. She wore a split tube top that showed off the piercing in her belly button and a pink hip-hugging skirt with an asymmetrical hem. She had let her perm grow out, and now her straight brown hair billowed in the afternoon breeze.

"Why is she following us?" Vanessa spoke in a hushed tone and fingered her hair nervously.

"We were asking the same question," Serena said.

"Oh look, it's Vanessa," Morgan called in a mocking voice.

Vanessa shook her head sadly. "I hate that we're going to have one more Follower to worry about, especially someone who used to be our friend."

"Speak for yourself." Catty made a face. "She was never my friend. You just don't remember how bad she was when she was normal."

Vanessa ignored Morgan's stare and concentrated on Cassandra. "Do you think she could suddenly have enough power to be a threat to us?

I mean she acts like she's got some big secret plan. Maybe I should follow her, you know, invisible."

Jimena smiled at her bravery. That was Vanessa's gift. She could expand her molecules and become invisible, but when she became really emotional she lost control and her molecules began to act on their own. When Vanessa had first started dating Michael, she had started to go invisible every time he tried to kiss her.

"Don't do anything yet," Jimena cautioned. "Not until we know more."

Vanessa nodded.

Serena started to stand. "I guess we're not going to fight them today."

"Is that what you're reading from them?" Catty asked.

"No, my bus is coming." Serena picked up her cello case.

"I'm going with you." Vanessa dug into her purse for her student bus pass.

"To my cello lesson?" Serena looked bewildered.

"No." Vanessa hesitated as if she wasn't sure

she wanted to tell them where she was going. "Okay, I'm going to see Michael. He's been a little too possessive lately, and I want to talk to him about it after he practices with his band today."

"A little too possessive?" Catty asked. "I thought you liked the way he was so attentive."

"I feel like I can't breathe." Vanessa looked down. "I just want time for myself."

The bus pulled up and Serena and Vanessa climbed on.

Catty watched the bus pull away. "I wonder if I'll ever have a boyfriend. It seems so unfair. You had Veto, and Serena had that guy last year. I'll probably never have someone."

"At least you're not one of those desperate girls who's willing to date some mutt just so she can go out."

They started walking through the crowd.

"I still wish I had a boyfriend even if it ended in total disaster. I feel so left out and lonely. Maybe I should go back a few years and trick some guy into falling for me," she giggled.

"You don't need to do that." Jimena punched her arm playfully.

Catty had the freakiest power of all. She could actually go back and forth in time. She missed a lot of school because of it. Her mother didn't care, though, because she knew Catty was different. She also wasn't Catty's biological mother. She'd found Catty walking along the side of the road in the Arizona desert when Catty was six years old.

"You'll find someone," Jimena tried to cheer her. "Next time we're at Planet Bang, stop watching your feet and look at all the guys who are looking at you."

Catty smiled.

Jimena turned back and looked at Cassandra, Karyl, and Morgan before they turned the corner.

The grim look on Cassandra's face brought on a premonition. Jimena gasped as the picture struck savagely. She saw Veto clearly, but she couldn't tell if it was nighttime or day. He was standing in MacArthur Park looking at Jimena. Then suddenly Cassandra came out from behind

Jimena, her hands reaching for Veto. Turbulent emotions came with the picture and Jimena clutched Catty for support. Was Cassandra embracing Veto or shoving him? Either way, the mental picture of the two of them together frightened her. She knew Cassandra was going to do something horrible.

CHAPTER FOUR

A ROLL OF THUNDER woke Jimena. She sat up in bed with a jerk, remembering the earthquake warning they had issued on TV. She glanced at her venetian blinds. They hung motionless. How could the thunder be an earthquake? Even the smallest *temblores* made her blinds sway, and there had been no pop and crack of the wooden door frames that always foretold the shaking of the earth. Maybe she had slept through those sounds, but she didn't think she could have. The Northridge quake had made all Angelenos super-sensitive to unnatural nocturnal sounds.

She stretched, then cuddled her pillow. The air felt chilly, and she tried to fold herself deeper under the covers. Rain hit the side of the apartment with a sudden gust.

She turned over and looked at the clock on her dresser. It read 3:00 A.M. There wasn't much chance she was going to go back to sleep now. Maybe a glass of milk would help. She tossed the covers aside and trundled down the dark hallway to the kitchen.

The apartment seemed too cold. She rubbed her arms and started to turn on a light to check the thermostat, when a sudden sound made her cautious. She flattened against the wall and held her breath. The soft clanking repeated.

She crept soundlessly down the hallway and peered into the kitchen. The window over the sink was open. The curtains billowed out and the wind drove the slanting rain inside. Her grandmother was too careful to leave a window open. Jimena looked carefully around the room. The neon signs outside cast eerie colored light into the room, and the undulating curtains made shadows roll over the table and cupboards.

She didn't see anything. She stepped onto the cold linoleum and started across the kitchen to close the window, when something moved in the corner of her vision.

She held her breath and froze. On the other side of the table, someone was bent over, going through a bottom cupboard.

A *tecato* maybe. It wouldn't be the first time some drug user had crawled up the rusted fire escape and broken inside looking for something to sell quickly for drug money.

She took a quiet step backward, grabbed a cast-iron skillet from the stove, and wrapped her fingers tightly around the handle. She held it up as a weapon and with her free hand turned on the overhead light. For a brief moment the glaring white glow blinded her.

Then the person turned. Jimena drew in her breath with a gasp.

CHAPTER FIVE

"JIMENA." VETO STOOD slowly, eyes blinking. He seemed uncomfortable. "Turn off the light."

In the brightly lit kitchen, she could see him more closely than she had the night before. She had the oddest impression that he was embarrassed to have her see him dressed the way he was, in a tight black T-shirt, too-long rumpled jeans, and tennis shoes that were obviously too big for his feet. She could smell detergent and fabric softener, and she had the inexplicable impression that he had stolen the clothes from a Laundromat or stripped them off a clothesline. The clothes dangled peculiarly on his body and looked unlike anything Veto had ever worn before.

He glanced at the frying pan raised in her hand, squinted, and tried to smile. "Still the tough one?" He didn't wait for her answer. "I didn't mean to scare you. I was going to wake you. I should have, but I remembered your grand-mother's cooking. Her *tamales* are the best in the world." He pointed to the empty corn husks piled on the kitchen table.

Crumbs covered the slick oilcloth. A jar of *jalapeños* sat open next to a dish filled with her grandmother's chunky sauce of tomatoes, cilantro, onions, and peppers. A ghost couldn't eat, could it? Surely that was proof he was real.

"I was just looking in the cupboard for something to clean up the mess I made." He stepped closer to her.

"You should have gotten me up." Her voice sounded angry, but she felt more hurt than angry. Since when did he need food more than he needed her?

He took the frying pan from her hand and set it back on the stove with a soft clank, then reached behind her and switched off the overhead light. The kitchen was bathed with the throbbing pink-and-blue neon lights from outside.

Veto's arm stayed behind her as he pressed her against the wall. He was still wet from the rain, and the sudden damp cold hit her with a sweet shock. His closeness made her forget all the questions she had wanted to ask him as her body filled with the delicious reality of holding him tight against her. She closed her eyes. If this was a dream or a fantasy, she didn't care. She didn't ever want it to stop.

After a long moment, she whispered against his ear, "Veto, I missed you so much. You have to tell me where you were."

"I missed you, too, baby." He rested his lips on her cheek.

"I hate you for leaving me alone." The words were spoken before she could stop them, but the tone with which she said them was more a confession of love.

"I know," he murmured and kissed her neck as if he were trying to kiss away her pain.

They were silent, enjoying the closeness of their bodies.

Veto spoke first. "I know how bad I hurt you."

"How? Were you watching me?" Her fingers trembled, unsure, as they worked their way up his arms to his shoulders.

"Every day." The words tickled against her ear.

"Why couldn't you have told me you were alive? You could at least have sent me a note." She couldn't say more. Her words were suddenly caught in the tumultuous emotions that tightened her throat.

"I was away."

She swallowed and forced her words out. "Away? Why'd you make us all think you were dead?"

"I'm sorry. There wasn't any other way. If there had been—"

"How can I believe you?" More than anything

she wanted to believe him. "You know how much I liked you." She had started to say *loved you*, but her hurt wouldn't allow her to say such a powerful word. She closed her eyes. Maybe it was a dream, only a dream, and he would fade away soon.

Veto pulled back and traced his fingers up her arm and across her shoulder to her lips. "Why are you smiling?"

"I'm laughing at myself," she answered without opening her eyes. "Because I'm wasting all this anger and pain and longing on you and you're probably nothing but a figment of my imagination."

"Can a dream do this?"

He pressed his lips on hers and the warm touch sent a jolt through her. She took in a quick breath, then slowly let her lips open. His tongue traced across her mouth and he pressed hard against her. His arms worked around her back and held her tight.

He pulled away and spread his fingers through her hair. "I promised you I'd never let anything separate us. You remember when I told you?"

She nodded and held up her hand. She still wore the thin gold ring he had given her that day. That was the day she had promised that she would be his someday.

He kissed the tips of her fingers. "I kept my promise. It was just hard to get back to you."

"From where?" she asked again. Wasn't he ever going to tell her? "Let me know what happened to you."

Thunder hammered across the night. The sound made the china vibrate in the cupboards. Jimena drew back and looked over Veto's shoulder. The curtains weren't swaying, and the leaves on the plants weren't bobbing.

"It can't be an earthquake," she said, more to herself than to Veto. Then she glanced at Veto. Even in the dim light she could see the look of sudden fear on Veto's face.

"What is it?" she asked, feeling her own heart race.

"Nothing." He tried to cover up his fear. He

put on his stone cold *máscara* as he'd always done in the old days when he faced down enemy gangsters, but he couldn't hide what was in his heart.

"You've never been afraid of anything—" she began.

"I'm not afraid—"

"Don't lie to me. I know you too well. I saw your face."

He hesitated. "It's the *temblores*. Since *el* Northridge I can't stand them. They make me crazy."

She could feel the falseness of his words. "You're lying to me," she repeated accusingly. "We never lied to each other before."

He tried to pull her back to him. "*Terremotos* have always scared me. You know they have."

She shook her head. "How come you feel afraid now?"

His hands dropped to his side, defeated. "I know what fear is now." He spoke the words so softly, she could barely hear them.

"Everyone knows what fear is! You think I'm *tonta*? Why'd you give me such a stupid answer?"

"I gave you the truth."

Another roll of thunder broke through the night.

"I gotta go." His words came out with a staccato quickness and his eyes darted around as if he were expecting someone to appear suddenly.

She clutched his arm tightly.

He looked at her oddly. "I have to leave now."

"Don't." Jimena held on to his arm, but already she could feel him pulling away from her. "Why are you running away just like the other night? Is someone after you?"

"Don't worry about it." He turned.

"Wait." She didn't want him to leave. She was afraid that if he did, she would never see him again. "I can help you. Tell me."

"I can't now. No time."

"Why don't you spend the night here?" She was frantically searching for a way to make him stay. Her voice sounded desperate.

He shook his head.

"Then promise me you'll meet me at school

the way you used to meet me at my old school, so I can show you off to my new friends."

"Where are you going to school now?" His eyes looked distracted and nervous. He kept glancing behind him at the open window. What was he looking for?

"La Brea High." She grabbed his hand. "Promise you'll be there."

"I promise."

A flood of light from the hallway filled the kitchen. She turned around as her grandmother walked into the room and turned on the overhead light. Jimena blinked and let her eyes adjust to the brightness.

"Jimena, who you talking to so late at night?"

"Veto," she started to say, but before the word left her mouth she turned back. The kitchen was empty.

Her grandmother walked across the small room and slammed the window, then grabbed a rag from under the sink and began wiping up the puddles on the floor before Jimena could see if there were any footprints in the water other than her own.

"What were you doing up?" Her grandmother's long braid fell over her shoulder as she worked.

"I guess I was walking in my sleep." Jimena looked at the window. Did she expect Veto to appear at the window and smile back at her?

She touched the side of her head. It was still wet from his hair. Or had that only been part of a dream?

"Let me fix you some cocoa so you can go back to sleep." Her grandmother stood and threw the rag under the sink. "I need some, too. Those *temblores* make me a bundle of nerves."

"You think the scientists are right?" Jimena sat down slowly, still dizzy from all the thoughts spinning through her head. "It didn't feel like an earthquake."

"It didn't feel right to me either." Her grandmother shrugged and started heating the water. "But scientists say so and I guess they know."

Her grandmother set a mug in front of her

and one on the opposite side of the table for her-self.

"Maybe I shouldn't go down to San Diego tomorrow?" Her grandmother threw tablets of chocolate into the water and began stirring.

"I'll be fine," Jimena answered the look of concern on her grandmother's face.

"You come with me, *m'ija*. Your grades are good now. You need time away from Los Angeles and you could help."

"I can't," Jimena lied. "I've got too many tests coming up."

Secretly she was glad her grandmother was going to San Diego. She felt that things with Cassandra and Karyl were going to become dangerous, and she didn't want to have to worry about her grandmother on top of everything else.

"All right, then." Her grandmother nodded. "I'll take the early Greyhound to San Diego tomorrow. I've been worrying about what your uncle has been doing to my recipes for a long time now. Better to act, eh? I'll go down there and see for myself."

"Better to do something than to worry," Jimena agreed and started making plans of her own. She'd wait for Veto tomorrow. She needed to know if he was real or not. She rubbed her head. Were her feelings for Veto so strong that she was conjuring up his ghost?

CHAPTER SIX

GEOMETRY CLASS SEEMED to drag on forever. Jimena kept glancing at the clock until Mr. Hall scowled at her. "Do you think you can help the clock move faster by watching it, Jimena?"

"No, sir." She stifled a yawn and looked at Catty.

Catty drew a chain of entwined roses and hearts across her notebook. Jimena thought she was a talented artist.

Vanessa still took notes, her pencil scratching across the paper at an impossible speed. She eagerly raised her hand to answer Mr. Hall's questions.

The desk in front of Vanessa was empty. Serena had cut afternoon classes. Jimena wished now she had gone with her. She needed to talk to her about Veto, but she had a suspicious feeling that Serena was meeting Stanton. Jimena felt nervous about it. She worried that whatever Cassandra was planning involved Stanton.

She tried to quiet her apprehension by listening to the steady tap of rain against the windows. The weather forecast said it would clear by this afternoon. She hoped so. She didn't want to wait in the rain for Veto.

The bell rang and she jumped.

Catty looked up and stretched as slow as a cat.

Vanessa had a satisfied grin and carefully tucked her notes inside her geometry book. "You guys want help with the homework?" Where did she get the energy?

"No," Catty and Jimena answered together.

Vanessa winked. "All right, but if you change your minds . . ."

"No!" Catty and Jimena shouted and followed Vanessa outside to the hallway.

"Look who's there." Catty pointed, then pulled on her yellow slicker and opened an umbrella. "I thought you asked him for breathing room?"

Michael leaned against a bank of lockers. His black hair was pulled back in a ponytail, accenting his strong, angular features. He smiled when he saw Vanessa and his dark eyes seemed to light up. No girl could resist looking at him. Vanessa had liked him since the beginning of the school year when she first met him in Spanish class. Jimena didn't understand why she suddenly felt like she needed more room. Michael didn't seem like the smothering kind of guy.

"I was hoping we could talk some more," he said to Vanessa. Without asking he took her books so that she could pull on her trench coat, then he put his arm around her and started guiding her away from Catty and Jimena.

"I'll see you guys later," Vanessa called over her shoulder.

"Can you believe she's got such a gorgeous guy and she's going to throw him away?" Catty opened her locker and put her geometry book inside.

"She's not throwing him away. She just wants more time for herself."

Catty nodded. "Still."

"I know . . ." Jimena agreed and longingly watched Vanessa and Michael walk away. "They look so in love."

"She's a dope if she lets him go." Catty slammed her locker.

"Sounds like you're a little *celosa*."

"A *little* jealous?" Catty grinned. "I'm crazy jealous. That's the one thing I want, and I don't ever think I'm going to get it." Catty looked down at her watch. "I'm late. I'm watching the shop for my mom this afternoon."

Catty's mother owned the Darma Bookstore on Third Street. Business had been slow recently, and Kendra had started teaching extension courses at UCLA. Catty's mother was a Latin scholar and had even worked once translating medieval manuscripts. She taught Latin and Classics. Jimena had been impressed when she met her. Kendra didn't seem the type to have done so much studying.

"So, you want to hang out at the store with me?" Catty asked. "We could make some tea and watch videos. It's never that busy. I think everybody in L.A. has their supply of Buddha beads." Besides prayer beads, the bookstore also sold candles, incense, crystals, and essential oils.

Jimena slipped into her coat. "No, I have something I have to do."

They waved good-bye, and Jimena walked out to the edge of campus, carrying a pile of books and an umbrella.

She sat on a cement bench that faced the street. The storm had started to clear, and blue sky peeked between swift moving clouds. A light breeze brought the smells of wet dirt, eucalyptus leaves, and drying cement. She lifted her hair and stretched, enjoying the feel of the clean air.

After an hour had passed, the sky had cleared completely. Jimena had missed one bus already, and when the next one approached she felt a need to run to it. Instead she let it roll by and decided to walk down to Beverly Boulevard and grab a bus there. She gathered her books and started walking.

She had only gone a little way when she felt a car pull up behind her. She turned expectantly, hoping to see Veto's smiling face, and was immediately let down.

Serena's brother, Collin, waved from behind the wheel of his utility van. Jimena had really disliked Collin when she first met him. Their constant bickering had upset Serena, but they got along okay now.

She stepped to the van and looked through the passenger-side window.

"I'm looking for Serena. Have you seen her?" His face was sunburned, his nose peeling and his lips still had traces of white zinc oxide. Lines from dried salt water traced around the back of his deeply tanned neck. Wind whipped through the driver's side window and blew his long white-blond hair into his blue eyes. He looked like something from a kid's comic book.

"I haven't seen her," Jimena answered.

"You haven't?" He looked surprised.

"Maybe she had a cello lesson," Jimena offered, even though she knew that wasn't true. Serena was keeping her relationship with Stanton a secret from Collin. Her brother was overly protective of his little sister, and that meant he tended to scare boyfriends away. Although, Jimena couldn't imagine anyone frightening Stanton.

"You want a ride then?" Collin leaned over and opened the passenger-side door.

She hesitated. There was still a chance she could meet up with Veto.

"Come on," he coaxed.

Finally she handed him her books and crawled in.

He smiled broadly and waited for her to hook the seat belt before he pulled away from the curb. His surfboard was in the back of the van wrapped in towels.

"Why aren't you surfing?" she asked. Collin was a total board-head. Waves were the only thing he ever had on his mind.

"Heavy rains bring pollution." He shrugged. "They closed the beaches."

During heavy rains, raw sewage filled with bacteria spilled into the ocean, threatening swimmers with hepatitis. But Jimena knew that not all of the beaches were closed. She had heard kids at school talking about the six-foot swells down at Huntington Beach.

"Too bad, storm surf is awesome." He mused. "You want to stop at Farmers' Market?"

"What for?"

"To get something to eat. Aren't you hungry?" He smiled and turned the wrong way. "Let's go down to Philippe's and grab a sandwich."

She shook her head. "Thanks, but I need to get home." The day felt so over for her. She just wanted to change into her sweats and go over her geometry while huddled in bed.

He continued driving toward downtown.

"You'll need to turn back," she reminded him. "I really don't have time today. Sorry."

He seemed disappointed. Maybe he hadn't eaten all day.

"Take this street back to Wilshire." She pointed and he took a quick right.

When they drove past MacArthur Park, Jimena thought she caught of glimpse of Cassandra.

"Pull over!" she yelled.

"Here?" Collin seemed surprised, but he was already aiming the car to the side of the road. "What's up?"

"I think I saw someone," she answered and unhooked her seat belt.

As the car slowed she jumped out and ran through the gridlocked traffic to the park. She hurried around people selling homemade food from large white kettles and darted past vendors' displays of brightly colored plastic toys, beaded jewelry, and silver watches.

She stopped near a man selling balloons and cotton candy in plastic bags.

Morgan and Karyl sat on a park bench near the lake, watching Cassandra step onto one of the paddleboats.

The wind twisted Cassandra's frilly lace skirt tightly around her.

Jimena started to go closer to investigate, when a commotion made her turn back. People were spilling from the sidewalks into the street, stopping traffic near Collin's van.

She glanced back at the water.

Cassandra sat down in the paddleboat, and Karyl and Morgan waved good-bye to her.

A shout made Jimena whip around and look back across the street. A young lanky boy climbed on the hood of Collin's van. He jumped up and down and waved his arms as if he had just won a soccer game.

She took one last glance at Cassandra. She was pedaling the boat out to the middle of the lake.

Then Jimena turned and sprinted back across the park. When she got to the other side of Wilshire near the van, she shoved through the crowd. She recognized some of the faces of the boys who were bothering Collin. Two lived in her grandmother's apartment building. They were acting bolder than their years, taunting Collin with lewd hand signs.

Collin leaned against the side of his van, legs crossed in front of him. He didn't seem worried. He was actually smiling at the boys.

The boys weren't Ninth Street and that was the problem. She thought they might belong to Wilshire 5. She had seen their graffiti in her grandmother's basement.

Collin didn't move. He was making no attempt to get back in his van and drive away. Didn't he know how dangerous this could be? Their spindly arms and legs might make them look like elementary school boys, but if he pushed them they would have to make a big show of their daring.

"*Hey,*" she let the word come out hard and severe.

The three boys turned slowly and faced her. Their shaved heads made them look too young for the violence that was on their minds.

"Hey, what?" the lanky one said.

Then all three boys moved as one, close together toward her, emboldened by one another's bravado.

Jimena shook her head and smiled. "You think the three of you make a *vato* strong enough to take me on?" She folded her arms carelessly over her chest.

The fat, dark boy with the long Lakers T-shirt and huge Nikes glared at her.

She knew instinctively that to win she had to act crazy. She let her hand reach inside her coat. She no longer carried a knife or a gun, but her hand remembered the motions of reaching under a shirt, and resting fingers on the cold heavy metal of a gun. That was dangerous. The boys could be strapping. Twelve- and thirteen-year-old kids could buy guns, or steal guns as easily as they could find a way to get a pack of cigarettes.

"Where you from?" The larger boy held his head up in challenge.

She laughed. "*Nueve. ¿Y qué?* I'm Ninth Street and so what? What do you think the three of you are going to do about it?"

The boys hadn't expected her to be ganged up. They were too young to remember the time when everyone knew Jimena.

For a moment the boys had a strange look on their faces and they exchanged tense glances. Jimena knew that they saw something menacing and *peligroso* in her eyes.

The larger boy stepped back. "Come on," he ordered. "*La chica no vale la pena.* She's not worth it."

The smaller one spit near her shoe before he turned and slowly followed his friend.

"Bitch," the lanky one mumbled under his breath. He turned and bumped against the people circling the van as he walked away.

Once they were away from Jimena, they sprinted across the street to the park. They stole a soccer ball from a group of younger boys and started to play a hard game to undo the humiliation that a *verdadera* gang member had just inflicted on them.

She looked at Collin and shook her head.

He was still smiling. Those boys probably couldn't have driven his car, but the posturing, pretending to be able to do it, was what amused them. Other twelve-year-old kids in her neighborhood were fighting a war. She remembered the helpless feeling of hearing gunshots and seeing the white flashes from the back of cars and diving for cover. That had been in the old days of drive-bys. Now gangsters got their 9-millimeters, walked uninvited into parties, and shot at point-blank range.

She knew what a bullet could do, and she suddenly felt angry that Collin hadn't gunned the motor and fled.

"You think this is so funny?" she snapped. Before she could say more, thunder rippled through the air.

People in the park glanced up and looked at each other with astonished faces. Some laughed with nervousness, but no one ran because there hadn't been a tremor.

She scanned the lake for Cassandra. The boat was gone, and Morgan and Karyl were no longer sitting on the park bench. She checked the rest of the park. She didn't see them, but in the commotion they could have seen her and hidden. If they were doing something for the Atrox, they wouldn't want her to know about it.

"Doesn't seem like a quake to me," Collin said beside her.

She couldn't forget her anger that quickly. "Why'd you stay and mess with those 'hood rats?"

Her anger took him by surprise. "What do you mean mess with them? They accosted me."

"You know what I mean," she said. "You should have gotten the hell out. You think you can face down a gang of little punks? They get out of control and have to show the others that they got what it takes even if they don't. It's like these punks can't wait to build a big reputation so everyone will know their name."

"Is that what you did?"

That caught her by surprise.

"Yeah," she whispered in a hoarse voice that seemed to travel over all the memories of the things she had done. She gathered her books from the front seat of his van.

His eyes had a new look for her. Was it pity,

embarrassment, or understanding? She pretended not to see, and went on, "Maybe one of them even had a gun." She turned and started walking toward her grandmother's apartment. "Why am I wasting my time? You've had a nice easy life, so there's no way you can understand."

"And you don't understand my philosophy." He walked along beside her.

She glanced up at him. "Your what?"

"No fear," he whispered.

"What's that supposed to mean?"

"If I had given in and run like you'd wanted me to, then fear would have taken hold inside me." He shrugged. "Then it starts to grow until you're afraid of every little kid who comes up to you dressed like a gangster."

"Maybe you *should* be afraid of those little kids." She held her books tight against her chest.

He shook his head. "Once you're afraid of something, you attract it into your life. I know."

"Don't be stupid."

"Yeah, you try to avoid it," he explained. "And you try to get away from it, and because you're trying so hard, you're always concentrating on it, and the more you concentrate on it, the more you pull it into your life."

She looked at him and wondered what he had feared that had made him develop such an odd philosophy. He seemed to read her thoughts.

"When I was younger my mother kept threatening to leave us." He looked away from her then. "I was afraid she would. The fear became huge inside me. Every day I ran home from school. Every day I cleaned my room. All I could think of was her leaving. I tried everything I could to make her stay, and then she left. That's when I decided to stop being afraid."

"You were just a kid then."

"So was Serena," he added. "But I knew from that day that fear is a wasted emotion. It never stops anything bad from happening."

"Do you know where your mother is?" Jimena asked quietly.

He shook his head. "Who cares? That was more than ten years ago." But she knew from the tone of his voice that he did care.

She stopped at the walk that led up to her grandmother's apartment building. "I don't know where my mother is either."

He glanced down at her.

"She never threatened to leave," Jimena added. "One day she was just gone. Drugs made her go."

"I'm sorry," he murmured.

"My grandmother told me that some people can't overcome their addictions and they should be pitied and prayed for and loved all the more—"

He interrupted her. "But you can't forgive her?"

She nodded. "It's worse than that. Even now, if I think about her, I can't remember her face. I only see the photographs my grandmother has shown me and instead of remembering the time I spent with her, I remember the stories my grandmother has given me to go with the photos."

"At least you had a reason for her leaving." Collin didn't seem to be speaking to her but to himself. "I wish I knew why mine left."

"Did your dad ever tell you?"

He laughed, but it was a dry unhappy sound. "Yeah, he said she wanted to be a movie star."

He walked her slowly up to the steps between the two cement lions. He stopped her before she put the key in the lock.

"That wasn't fair what I said, about how at least you know why your mother left. It had to hurt as badly as mine leaving." He touched her hand. It surprised her and brought on a premonition so strong that she uttered a small cry and fell back off the step.

He caught her arm. "What?" he asked. "Are you okay? Why are you looking at me so strangely?"

She had seen herself kissing Collin. And it hadn't been a brotherly peck on the cheek. The kiss was long and passionate. She brushed her fingers across her lips. Collin? Why would she ever kiss Collin?

"Sorry," she said and fumbled with the key. It kept sliding across the lock. "I don't know what came over me."

He took the key from her, inserted it into

the lock, turned the knob, and handed the key back to her. "Maybe it hurt too much to talk about your mother."

She started to go inside. "No, that was okay. Sometimes it's good to talk about the bad things. It makes them hurt less."

He nodded and she closed the door, then stood to the side, and watched him walk back to his van.

She needed to see Maggie. Something had to be wrong with her power. First she had seen Cassandra with Veto and she wasn't even sure if Veto was alive or dead. And now she had a premonition of kissing Collin, her best friend's brother. She supposed it was possible for her power to mess up. It had happened once when she had a head cold and lost her hearing and sense of smell. Maybe standing in the rain had given her some kind of illness that had affected her.

This was definitely an emergency. She turned abruptly and ran up the stairs to her grandmother's apartment. She felt too impatient to wait for the elevator.

She unlocked the door, dropped her books on the floor, and picked up the phone. She had just started to dial when someone grabbed her from behind. She turned around, swinging.

CHAPTER SEVEN

VETO STOOD BEHIND HER, holding his jaw. "You hit hard," he teased.

"Veto! You scared me to death." She wanted to be angry with him but she felt too happy to see him. "How did you get in here, anyway?"

"The kitchen window." He handed her a single red rose.

She took it, sniffed the sweet fragrance, and made a mental note to nail the window shut.

She tilted her head in a flirty way and looked Veto up and down.

He wore a black leather jacket over a plaid

button-up shirt and khakis. A gold earring glistened in his ear and he had gotten a haircut. He smiled as if he knew she was admiring the way he looked.

"I couldn't meet you at school." He touched her chin lightly. "I had things to do."

She rolled her eyes. "What else is new?"

He took her hand and pulled her toward the door. "But now I have time. Come on. This is the first time it hasn't been raining. Let's go to the park so I can tell you everything."

"Everything?" She looked up at him, expectant.

"Yeah," he said as he opened the door. "*Todo*—and I'll answer all your questions too."

She set the rose down and grabbed her keys.

As they walked toward the park, Jimena felt as if a terrible worry were being lifted from her shoulders. People smiled at Veto and said hello. Three little boys ran up to him and asked if he wanted to buy candy bars for their Little League. There was no doubt in her mind now that he was real. She leaned against him as they walked down the crowded street. She wondered how she could have ever thought he was a ghost.

"When are you going to tell me?" she murmured.

"Soon," he promised. "Wait till we get to the park. Right now I can't get enough of this sunshine."

"I know." She lifted her face to the sun and enjoyed its warmth.

Children in bathing suits and shorts jumped in the rain puddles that shimmered gold.

They crossed the street through the gridlocked rush-hour traffic and entered the park. A *tecato* drifted toward them, his heroin-thin bony hand shaking a cup at them. His few begged coins rattled at the bottom.

Veto stared at the addict, then shook his head sadly. His reaction surprised Jimena. In the old days he might have yelled at or lectured the man.

Jimena turned and looked up at Veto. There was something different about him but she couldn't quite put her finger on it.

A woman wrapped in a *rebozo* sat on a beach chair with a bag of mangoes between her feet. Veto handed her a dollar. She took a knife, cut the mango into six easy slices, dropped the slippery yellow pieces into a sandwich bag, and handed it to Veto.

He gave one to Jimena and took one himself.

Veto took a bite and the juice ran down his chin. He didn't try to wipe it away but closed his eyes and held his face up to the sun. "This is heaven, you know. Sunshine and mango and you." His eyes opened and he looked at her in a strange way as if he were trying to memorize every thing about her.

"Kiss me," he whispered.

She leaned over and kissed his sweet lips.

"Let's go watch the old men play chess." He took a handkerchief from his back pocket, wiped his hands, and gave the hankie to Jimena. She wiped the sticky juice from her hands and face.

Veto took her hand and pulled her to the corner of the park where the old men had set up chairs and tables. They were hunched over, concentrating on the checkered boards. In the old days Veto liked to come here and watch the men play and then whisper their mistakes into Jimena's ear.

They stood behind an old man wearing a *tandito* and Stacy Adams shoes. His tattooed hand hovered over the castle. Age had blurred the letters written in his skin.

Veto studied the board.

Jimena felt a change in her moon amulet and looked up. Her breath caught. Karyl and Morgan were five feet away, their backs to her. They apparently hadn't sensed her presence because they were concentrating on the lake. Were they waiting for Cassandra? She shielded her hands against the glare on the water. The geyserlike fountain in the center continued spraying water, but she didn't see any paddleboats. The pedalo boat ride looked closed.

"*Oye*," Jimena whispered to the old man with his hand on the chess piece. "When do the boat rides open?"

The old man looked up at her, annoyed.

"Domingo, solamente domingo." He looked back at the chessboard.

"You want to go for a ride?" Veto asked. "The boat rides are only open on Sunday, but I can steal one."

Had Cassandra stolen a paddleboat?

She glanced back at Karyl and Morgan. She didn't need a premonition to know they were up to something bad. Her moon amulet vibrated against her chest in warning.

Veto could always read her emotions. Already he was scanning the park, trying to see what she saw. He put his arm around her and pulled her closer to him. "What? You see something? Wilshire 5?"

"I don't bang hard anymore. It's something else. You wouldn't understand." She caught the look on his face. He didn't like being excluded from her thoughts.

"Dime. Tell me."

The two men playing checkers sensed the command in Veto's voice and looked up.

"Nothing." She tried to make her voice

sound carefree. "I'm just getting a headache maybe from all the sun."

Veto recognized the lie. "*La verdad*, Jaguar. Tell me the truth. I've seen too much now for you to keep anything from me. *Ojalá*, more than you'll ever have to deal with or see." His eyes looked tired now. "Anything that's bothering you, you can tell me."

"I see some people I don't like." That was true, even though it wasn't the complete truth.

"If they give you trouble, I'll take care of them," he promised. "You know I will."

"This is a different kind of trouble," she whispered, her voice low with warning.

"*No hay nada* I can't handle." He spoke it like a solemn oath.

She nodded. There had been a time when that was true. Was it still? Could he help her find out why Karyl and Morgan were waiting by the lake? Maybe he could go over and talk to them, distract them while she had a chance to get in closer, and see if they were doing anything. But that was too dangerous. She would never risk Veto.

"So forget about them," Veto nudged her. "You're safe with me. Come on. I have important things I want to tell you. Let's go sit on a bench."

She started to follow him when thunder roared from the ground like a diesel truck bearing down on them at full speed. The ground shook and the vibrations traveled up her leg and through her back.

Veto grabbed Jimena and held her tightly against him.

All around them pandemonium broke loose. People ran away from trees, cars, and buildings, fearing this tremor might be the prelude to the big one.

Jimena glanced at Karyl and Morgan. They weren't running like the others. They stood and slowly walked to the edge of the lake. They were smiling as if the earth tremors had somehow made them happy.

The earth stopped shaking, but her heart was still beating wildly.

The water in the lake lapped at the sides and spilled over onto the asphalt path.

People laughed nervously. The two old men were picking up chess pieces and returning them to their chessboard.

"Ha, you'd do anything to get out of a losing match," the man in the *tandito* teased his friend.

The other old man smiled and picked up a knight from the dust.

Jimena remember how Veto had become so frightened before when he heard the earthquake thunder. She glanced up at him. He didn't seem afraid this time. She started to ask him why, but stopped.

The afternoon suddenly collapsed around her and she was filled with a cruel sense of déjà vu. Veto was standing exactly as he had stood in her premonition. She swirled around looking for Cassandra, afraid she was suddenly going to appear.

She shuddered. "Leave, Veto."

He looked confused. "I wanted to explain things to you."

She shook her head. "Go." The memory of Cassandra reaching for Veto closed in tight and she started to tremble.

"What?" Veto asked with true concern. "What's wrong?"

Everything seemed to move in slow motion around her as utter panic took hold. She looked behind her. How could she tell Veto about the premonition and make him understand how dangerous Cassandra was? Even if she could explain who Cassandra was, Veto would want to stay and fight.

She started to speak but her mouth felt too dry and she had to clear her throat first. "Things around here aren't the same as you remember them. There are other dangers."

He looked at her oddly, but he was still standing as he had been in her premonition.

Why wouldn't he go? Or at least, move. She shoved him hard, and still he didn't move.

"Jimena?" He reached out for her, filling her with an absolute sense of doom.

She felt suddenly trapped in a horrible dark hole even though she was standing in full sunlight. The sun now felt cold on her skin. She heard the stealthy snap of a footstep behind her and turned quickly. It was only a child trying to sneak up on a pigeon. She looked back at Veto.

"Veto, if you ever liked me, just do it. Just go. Please."

He took slow easy steps backward spreading his arms. "*Ya me voy*, all right? I'm going." He paused. "Where do you go with your friends?"

"What do you mean?" she said in a dry voice.

"Where do you hang out?" he continued as he took impossibly slow strides away from her. "Tell me so I can come see you."

"Friday night I'll be at Planet Bang."

"I'll see you there."

She nodded.

Jimena watched Veto run from her with a sigh of relief. He was far from her now, and she felt that he was safe again.

At last, she looked back at the lake. Karyl and Morgan were gone now. She scanned the park, but she didn't see them anywhere.

The sun was low on the horizon when she

finally walked back to her grandmother's apartment. She was going to call Maggie right away.

Jimena had picked up the phone and started to dial Maggie when someone knocked on the door.

She went to answer it. As soon as she opened the door, Serena, Vanessa, and Catty rushed inside with worried looks. Serena's tongue stud clicked nervously against her teeth.

"What?" Jimena looked from one to the other. She couldn't tell if they were angry or frightened or both.

Vanessa spoke first. "Tell Jimena what you told us."

Serena cleared her throat. "Stanton gave me a warning."

Catty kicked off her clogs and paced in chunky-striped socks that crawled up her pink tights. "I still don't understand why he would tell you. It has to be a set-up."

"Let her speak," Jimena broke in.

Serena stretched on the couch and cuddled a pillow.

"Because," Vanessa started to explain. "He uses us whenever someone threatens his position. I believe him. This isn't the first time he's told us something."

Catty walked over to the couch and fell on it. "I don't trust him."

"Tell Jimena," Vanessa coaxed Serena. "She can make up her own mind."

Serena began slowly, "Stanton told me that Cassandra has suddenly become favored by the most powerful Atrox Followers, the Cincti."

"Cincti?" Jimena translated the Latin. "Encircled? I don't understand."

"Cincti is what Followers call members of the Inner Circle," Serena explained.

Catty shook her head. "This is too much to believe."

Serena continued softly, her words heavy with concern, "In all the centuries that Stanton's been a Follower, he's never heard of anyone who is not an Immortal being allowed to visit the Inner Circle."

"Why would they choose Cassandra then?" Jimena asked. "She's definitely not an Immortal."

"That's my point exactly." Catty leaned forward. "Why Cassandra? I think Stanton's setting us up."

"I don't." Vanessa argued. "I think he uses us when it's to his advantage. And it's definitely to his advantage if we can stop Cassandra."

"He needs us to stop Cassandra," Serena said. "If Cassandra succeeds, then her place of power will be higher than his." Serena hesitated now as if she were trying to regain a measure of calm. "Cassandra wants revenge."

"She probably wants to get even with him for those ugly letters she cut into her skin." Catty nervously picked at the funky snake designs on her nails.

Jimena looked at Serena. Serena wasn't telling Catty and Vanessa the really bad news. Stanton had jilted Cassandra to be with Serena. Jimena could only imagine how much Cassandra wanted to get even with them both . . . if she knew. Maybe that's why the Regulators hadn't come after Stanton and Serena. Maybe Cassandra hadn't told the Atrox, because she was planning revenge on her own terms. Jimena shuddered and looked at Serena.

A worried look crossed Serena's face, but her voice was steady as she continued. "Stanton said she's been allowed to visit the Inner Circle because she has a fail-safe plan to stop the Daughters of the Moon."

"To stop *us*." Vanessa repeated the words for emphasis. "That's why she's been acting so nasty."

"Does Stanton know what her plan is?" Jimena asked.

Serena shook her head.

"Go on," Vanessa urged. "There's more."

Serena pulled a tube of lip balm from her pocket and rubbed it across her lips before she went on. "The Cincti have allowed her to go back into the past to change one event so she can start her plan in motion."

"Has she gone already?" Jimena's fingers went automatically to her amulet. She pressed it into her palm.

Serena nodded. "Whatever they changed, they've changed it already."

Jimena looked from Catty to Vanessa and back to Serena. "Does Stanton know what event she changed?"

"No." Serena shook her head. "But whatever it was, it worked, because she was able to set her plan in motion."

"That's one reason I don't believe Stanton," Catty put in. "You can't go back and change something unless it was always meant to be."

"What do you mean—you can't change time?" Jimena asked. "They already did."

"Because," Catty explained. "Time isn't like a river with one day following the next. We just think of it that way because that's the way we've been taught; everyone talks about tomorrow or yesterday, but really all time occurs at once."

"Yesterday and tomorrow happen at the same time?" Vanessa rolled her eyes. "That's impossible."

"No. How else can I go back and forth in time?" Catty asked. "It's because time is like a huge lake—it exists all at once. We just experience it one day at a time. That's why I can never do anything to change what has happened in the past. Because if I were going to change something, it would already be part of our experience. See? So Cassandra couldn't have changed something. It was something that was always meant to be."

They all stared at her dumbly.

Jimena thought a moment. "So you're saying, if Cassandra changed something in the past, because it is already *past*, as far as we're concerned it's not something that has been changed, because it already happened to us."

Catty smiled. "Yup."

"I'd still like to know what she did," Jimena said.

"Me, too," Vanessa agreed.

"So just supposing that what Stanton said is true, what are we going to do?" Serena asked.

"I can't believe you're buying into anything that a Follower said." Catty stood. "You got anything to eat? All this talk has made me hungry."

Soon, they were sitting around the table in the kitchen dipping fried tortillas filled with melted cheese into a pot of homemade salsa.

"So we need a plan," Vanessa said finally.

"Let's go see Maggie," Catty suggested.

"We always do that." Serena took another *quesadilla.* "Let's at least try to figure something out by ourselves first."

"Well," Jimena started. "I saw Karyl, Morgan, and Cassandra in MacArthur Park today."

"What were they doing this far from Hollywood?" Catty wondered.

"Do you think it has something to do with Cassandra's plan?" Serena asked.

"I don't know," Jimena answered. "Earlier today when I saw Cassandra she was stepping onto one of the paddleboats. That was odd, because the boat ride is closed on weekdays. It's only open on Sunday. And when I went back later, I didn't see Cassandra, only Karyl and Morgan. And remember the earthquake this afternoon?"

"It didn't feel like a quake," Catty put in.

"When we had the tremor, Karyl and Vanessa didn't get scared like everyone else, they seemed—" Jimena thought, trying to find the right word for the expressions she had seen on their faces.

"What?" Serena licked her fingers.

"They seemed happy or maybe excited, but not in a bad way," Jimena answered. "Everyone else was running and screaming, but they smiled as if they'd been looking forward to it."

"Could they have discovered a way to make an earthquake?" Vanessa didn't hide the amazement in her voice.

"Impossible." Catty rolled her eyes. "They were probably just hoping someone would get hurt."

"Still the Inner Circle would be really powerful. . . ." Serena let her words trail off. "Do you think?"

"Maybe we should stake out the park," Jimena suggested. "And see if we can discover what Cassandra is up to."

Serena nodded in agreement.

"That's a good idea," Vanessa said. "I'll bring a flashlight so we can study."

"Please." Catty playfully punched Vanessa. "Why do you have to ruin every adventure?"

"We have to get into a good college," Vanessa reminded her and then stopped.

Catty looked down at the table. "It seems kind of silly to study unless . . ."

"Unless what?" Vanessa asked.

Catty stared at her. "Unless you've already made your decision."

Vanessa blushed.

The girls looked at each other. Their gifts only lasted until they were seventeen. Then there was a change, a metamorphosis. They had to make the most important choice of their life. Either they could choose to lose their powers and their memory of what they had once been, or they disappeared. The ones who disappeared became something else, guardian spirits perhaps. No one really knew. They didn't like to think about it.

"Let's not start worrying about that now," Serena broke in.

"Yeah," Jimena agreed. "Let's concentrate on the present."

"Okay, so let's start tonight," Vanessa suggested. "We'll camp right out there with all the drug dealers, addicts, and homeless people."

"Sounds like fun," Catty laughed.

"What else can we do?" Serena asked.

No one had an answer.

CHAPTER EiGHT

FRIDAY NIGHT, Serena was the first to arrive. She wore a slinky one-shoulder black dress with a plunging neckline and a beaded gold belt slung low on her waist. She carried a fringed bag, and Jimena suspected that her dangling earrings were a gift from Stanton.

"Wow," Jimena squealed, as she let Serena into her grandmother's apartment. "You're dressed to kill."

Serena seemed breathless with excitement. "What about you? I love that halter top with the split up the middle."

"Thanks." Jimena hurried back to the bathroom. She hadn't finished putting on her makeup yet.

A sly smile crossed Serena's face as she sat on the edge of the white porcelain tub. "Why are you fixing yourself up so special tonight? Are you meeting some hottie you haven't told me about?"

"I do this whenever we go out." Jimena rolled mascara on her lashes.

"You always look good, but tonight you look extra special. Maybe it's the glow of love," Serena teased.

Jimena bit her lip. She had been dying to tell Serena about Veto all week, but the right time never came. It seemed that Serena was always running off with Stanton, and if she and Serena had a moment together, Catty and Vanessa always showed up.

Jimena turned and faced her. "There is someone."

Serena gasped with delight. "I knew it. I've been picking up these dreamy thoughts from you all week of kissing and hugging, but I couldn't see who you were with."

"No fair reading my mind," Jimena said with a smile as she snapped crystals into her hair.

"Who are you going to see?" Serena stood.

Jimena looked back at the mirror and saw a blush rising to her cheeks, then she glanced at Serena's reflection.

Serena appeared perplexed. "Veto?! How?" Then her face became serious. "How are you going to meet Veto at Planet Bang? Are you having a séance?"

Someone knocked at the door.

"I'll explain later." Jimena hurried to answer the door.

Serena followed her. "Tell me."

"His ghost is still haunting me," Jimena teased mysteriously. She didn't have all the answers yet herself, so how was she going to explain Veto's sudden reappearance to Serena? "Let's talk later."

She opened the door and Catty and Vanessa pushed inside. Catty wore an iridescent hot green mini and matching eye shadow. Vanessa had covered herself with an ultrafine glitter. It looked really hot with her gold halter top. Her skirt hung across her flat stomach and hugged her hips.

"Tell her she needs to pierce her belly button if she's going to show off her body like that," Catty said as if she were continuing an argument they had started on the bus.

Vanessa ignored Catty. "Are we still planning to go to the park again tonight? It feels like such a waste of time. We haven't seen Cassandra all week."

"I think she knows about our plan and that's why we haven't seen her," Catty said.

Vanessa stared at Serena. "Did you tell Stanton that we were planning to stake out the park? He might have said something to Cassandra."

"I can't believe you'd think I'd tell Stanton our plan," Serena answered and toyed nervously with her new gold earrings.

"It's just strange Cassandra never showed up." Vanessa sighed. "I guess we should go to the park one last time."

"Dressed like this?" Catty asked.

"No one will see us if we're careful." Serena started toward the door.

Jimena followed her. "Yeah, and if some *tecato* does see us he'll just think he's having a heroin dream."

Vanessa stuck her hand into her gold velvet bag and pulled out a lipstick. She brushed it across her lips. "It's Friday already, and it just seems that if we haven't seen Cassandra once all week we're not likely to see her tonight. Besides, the moon is full. Do you really think she'd do anything during the full moon?"

The Daughters were more powerful under the steady glow of a full moon, but Followers were betrayed by the same light; their eyes turned phosphorescent and even ordinary people could sense their evil during that time.

"You just want to get to Planet Bang because you've made up with Michael again," Serena said accusingly.

"Would you stop reading my mind!" Vanessa tossed the lipstick back in her purse.

"What was all the big deal about needing breathing room?" Catty badgered.

Vanessa beamed. "We gave each other

breathing room, but then we missed each other too much."

"You mean you were afraid he'd get interested in someone else," Catty put in.

"Maybe." Then Vanessa looked at Jimena. "Seriously, do you think it's worth staking out the park one more time? Maybe we should just go on to Planet Bang."

"I think we should try one last time." Jimena opened the door.

"Yeah," Serena agreed. "Then we'll go see Maggie tomorrow."

The night was warm, with a gentle wind. They walked up Wilshire Boulevard under swaying shadows cast from the palm trees. As they neared the park Jimena noticed how each of them became quieter and started glancing at her moon amulet.

They hadn't gone far when they passed a guy removing the hubcap from his car. He looked suspiciously at Jimena, then stood and with the skill of a magician, swapped a small plastic bag for the bills wadded in the trembling hand of a man standing near him. Only someone who knew would have seen the transaction. Others would have thought the drug dealer was shaking the hand of a friend who had come to help him change a tire.

The full moon hung low in the eastern sky as they strolled into the park. Homeless people were starting to make beds for the night, laying out pieces of cardboard and claiming shelter under park benches.

Vanessa kicked aside a used hypodermic syringe. "I don't know what Followers could do to make the park worse."

Catty agreed. "What would they want to do here anyway?"

"It doesn't make sense, when they usually hang out in Hollywood." Serena added.

Jimena looked around. "The park's different during the day, when the old men and street vendors and children are here. It's a nice place then."

"Yeah, maybe the Followers have always claimed it at night," Catty suggested. "That could explain all the bad stuff that happens here after the sun goes down."

They stopped near the edge of the lake. Jimena's amulet began humming softly against her chest. "Look," she whispered.

Cassandra walked toward them, her hips swaying with practiced ease, and high-heeled boots clicking nicely on the asphalt path. A breeze blew through her long maroon hair as she tossed her head. She wore tight, low-cut jeans and a skimpy studded top. Silver chains dangled low on her hips. Under the moon's steady glow the jagged STA scars on her chest seemed to luminesce against her skin. Her eyes burned yellow.

A homeless man started to ask her for money but then drew back as if he had suddenly sensed her evil.

Jimena, Catty, and Vanessa quietly stepped into the shadows. Jimena had to pull Serena after them. Jimena felt a kind of nagging fear at the back of her mind as she watched silently. Her nerves tingled with anticipation.

Cassandra stood at the edge of the lake and

waited for a paddleboat to drift toward her.

"How did she do that?" Vanessa wondered. "The boats are all tied together."

Jimena shook her head "Maybe she didn't do it. Maybe the boat just got loose." But she knew that wasn't the case. She sensed that more was happening than they were seeing. She could feel the change in the air, something electrical and alive.

Cassandra stepped into the boat.

"Why's she doing that?" Catty asked in a low voice.

"That's what I saw her do that first day," Jimena whispered back. "The boat ride was closed, but she somehow found a stray boat and stepped on."

Cassandra rode the bobbing boat toward a geyserlike fountain.

Jimena was filled with frustration. Her muscles felt tight. "We can't see her if she goes behind the jet of water."

"I'm going to go invisible and follow her." Already Vanessa's molecules were starting to separate and she looked like a dusty cloud. The cloud swirled with a twinkle of gold, and then she became completely invisible.

Jimena could no longer see her, but she could feel a soft breeze as Vanessa flowed up and over her and headed toward the lake.

They waited impatiently in the shadows. Then a thought rose inside Jimena and she knew Vanessa was in danger. Her hands clasped into fists, and she started to run toward the lake as the ground began to tremble.

Thunder crashed through the air and the earth shook.

Jimena stopped. She glanced up and saw a golden burst of light over the lake. The light quickly became a dense form.

"Vanessa!" Jimena shouted with alarm.

Vanessa was visible again and tumbling quickly toward the water.

"Come on. Let's go help her!" Serena yelled, but Jimena was already running to the other side of the lake.

Just as Vanessa was about to hit the water,

her molecules separated into long strands and she became invisible again.

"She caught herself just in time." Catty panted as she came to a stop.

Serena slowed her pace. "Something bad must have happened to make her lose her concentration. Do you think Cassandra did something to her?"

"I hope she's all right," Jimena whispered.

A whirlwind whipped around them and then molecule by molecule Vanessa pulled herself back together until she was standing whole in front of them.

"What happened?" Catty asked.

"Cassandra disappeared." Vanessa caught her breath.

"What do you mean disappeared?" Jimena felt baffled. "How could she just disappear?"

Vanessa smoothed her hands over her body, straightening her halter and skirt. "Just that. She was there one minute and the next, both she and the paddleboat were gone. I wasn't expecting it, so I lost control and started falling toward the water."

The girls stared at each other.

"Does she have a special power like Vanessa's?" Catty wondered.

Serena shook her head. "I've never heard Maggie mention it. She would have told us. Some of the Followers are shape-changers, but those are all Immortals."

Vanessa interrupted. "You didn't let me finish." Her hand clasped Jimena's wrist. Her fingers were ice-cold.

"There's more?" Catty's eyes widened.

Vanessa nodded. "It didn't look like she became invisible. I would have understood what was happening if I'd seen her molecules spreading. It was just that she was there and then all of a sudden she was gone. As if she and the paddleboat had passed into another dimension."

They stared out at the moon's reflection on the lake.

Catty broke the silence. "So now we've seen Cassandra in the park, but can anybody figure out what she was doing?"

Vanessa shook her head.

"What we do know is that she's doing something odd here and that it involves the lake," Jimena said.

They all turned back and watched the shooting fountain in the middle of the water.

Serena nodded and stepped to the edge of the lake. "What's so important about this lake?"

"Beats me," Catty answered.

"The land here used to be a swamp," Jimena explained. "But the swamp was drained a long time back, and now the red-line subway tunnels under it, so the lake's bottom is actually the subway's roof."

Vanessa looked perplexed. "That doesn't sound like enough of a reason for Cassandra to be interested in it."

"Maybe it's what you said," Catty put in.

Vanessa turned to her, confused. "What?"

"Maybe she goes into another dimension. . . . Maybe there's a door or tunnel into another realm," Catty suggested.

"Could be," Vanessa answered.

"We can ask Maggie tomorrow," Serena suggested.

Finally, Jimena took a deep breath and sighed. "We might as well go on to Planet Bang. We're not going to get anything done here."

The girls started walking away from the lake. They didn't noticed the empty paddleboat bobbing back to the shore.

CHAPTER NINE

B Y THE TIME CATTY, Vanessa, Serena, and Jimena arrived at Planet Bang their mood had lifted. The music was loud and the resounding beat made them forget Cassandra.

"Look at the line," Catty moaned.

Kids were crushed against the building in a line four deep, waiting to be checked by the security guards before they went inside to buy their tickets. The line continued down the block.

"Forget the line." Jimena started walking quickly. "Follow me."

Serena hurried after her.

"Come on," Catty cried to Vanessa and grabbed her hand.

They ran past the security guards.

"Hey!" someone shouted.

They hurried inside and shoved into the crowd of kids waiting to pay their entrance.

A security guard yelled after them, "Come back here."

"We better go back." Vanessa glanced nervously behind her.

"Don't look back," Serena warned. "They'll see your face. They won't come after us and risk having that mob of kids break loose and run in here. You think they want a riot?"

"Still, it was wrong what we did," Vanessa sulked. "What if the security guards look for us after?"

"Loosen up, Vanessa," Catty laughed and paid her entrance fee. "With everything going on, do you think they really care that four hot chicks pushed past security without letting them dig through their purses?"

Vanessa smiled. "The line looked a mile

long. I really didn't want to wait in it."

"Now you've got it." Serena paid and they hurried inside.

The breakneck rhythm thumped through the walls and pulsed around them. Their bodies felt the need to move and they started to dance close, hips in line, the way they had practiced. Jimena scanned the crowd, searching for Veto.

"Hey, guys." Michael Saratoga came over to Vanessa and kissed her cheek. She smiled and followed him to the dance floor. Catty stopped dancing and watched them go.

Serena stopped, too, and peeked at her watch, then around the room. "I have something I have to check on." She didn't bother to wait for their reply but hurried off.

"Who's she trying to fool?" Catty asked.

"What do you mean?" Jimena stared after Serena as she disappeared into one of the dark corners where lodos and stoners hung out. Had Catty figured out why Serena was always disappearing and who she was meeting?

"I mean, it's so obvious she's meeting a guy."

Catty put her hands on her hips. "Don't you think? I mean, why doesn't she want us to see him? Is he some complete nerd or something? I've even thought that maybe she's seeing someone's boyfriend."

"She hasn't said anything to me." Jimena hated lying.

Catty looked at her suspiciously, then sighed. "When is it going to be my turn? I mean, you've had a boyfriend. Vanessa has too many guys who like her anyway, and now Serena's always running off to meet some secret hottie."

Jimena laughed.

"It's not funny." Catty pouted.

"Yeah, it is." Jimena started dancing. She took Catty's hand and danced with her back to the dance floor. "It's funny because you haven't bothered to check out what's around you."

"What do you mean?" Catty started moving, facing Jimena this time.

"Move your hips, wild one," Jimena teased. "And I'll show you."

"What?" Catty seemed baffled.

"You are way too cute to think you're never going to get a boyfriend." Jimena placed her hands on Catty's hips. They danced close, facing each other. Jimena glanced around. "Okay, now look at the guys watching us."

"I see them," Catty complained. "They're all looking at you."

"Not." Jimena laughed. "Now I want you to take a good look around and pick the one that you like."

Catty turned and studied the guys. A cryptic smile slowly blossomed on her face. She smoothed her hands up over her waist, up and around her neck, then slowly through her hair, as if she were testing her power over the guys.

Suddenly, she turned back and faced Jimena. She was blushing and breathless with excitement. "I sort of like the one with the spiky hair." Catty motioned over her shoulder with her chin.

Jimena looked around. "Chris?"

"Yeah." Catty smiled.

Chris was new at La Brea High. He was a sweet-looking guy with a sizzling smile, but

Jimena was surprised that he was the one Catty would pick from all the *rompecorazones* and golden boys who were staring at her. He wore extra-large long shorts that came to the tops of his white socks and a heavy-metal red leather belt with spiky studs. A large suede cuff was buckled around his wrist. His head bobbed to the music and his red leather Reeboks bounced up and down.

Jimena sighed. He looked . . . well . . . strange. She shrugged. "Okay." Then she danced Catty over to Chris.

He smiled shyly and pointed to his chest as if to say "Me?" When Catty nodded, his smile stretched into a look of happy surprise, and he started dancing with her.

Jimena watched them for a moment, then closed her eyes and let the music take her away. She lifted her hands over her head and swayed. Someone bumped into her. She didn't bother to open her eyes to see who it was, but continued moving with the beat.

This time the person pressed against her.

Warm hands snaked around her bare waist.

A pleasant nervousness rushed through her. She turned and started to murmur Veto's name, but his name caught in her throat. "Collin!" What was he doing at Planet Bang?

"Hi, Jimena."

She stared at him. There was something different about him. Then she knew—it was the first time she had seen him without traces of zinc oxide on his nose and lips. His sunburn had turned a deep bronze and his blond hair wasn't windblown, but combed and silky. She had never seen him look so good. Then the premonition of the passionate kiss flashed uninvited into her mind. She blushed and backed away from him.

He grabbed her hand and pulled her back. The air was fragrant with his tangy soap smell. "You want to dance?" She took a deep breath. She was filled with dizzy confusion. Why would Collin want to dance with her? He smiled. Was he flirting with her?

She shrugged and wished she had worn a sweater over her revealing top. She could feel his belt buckle pressing against her stomach. She couldn't catch her breath.

"Why do you look so surprised?" he asked.

She glanced up at him. Why hadn't she noticed how handsome he was before?

He held her close, his hands firm on the small of her back. She placed her hands on his chest and tried not to look in his blue eyes. Normally his eyes were rimmed with red from too much time in salt water, but tonight they were clear and deep.

He looked down at her, but she quickly looked away. Why couldn't she look into his eyes when it was usually so easy to look in the eyes of other guys, tilt her head, and tease them?

She continued dancing with him but felt uncomfortably aware of the closeness of their bodies, the scratch of his khakis on her bare legs.

His hands moved up to the exposed skin on her back and he leaned down, pressing his cheek next to hers. She didn't know what to do with her hands, which were awkwardly crushed between them, a barricade.

Someone tapped her shoulder. She turned quickly, grateful for an excuse to pull away from Collin. Her face felt flushed and she drew in air.

Catty spoke into her ear. "Thanks. Chris is so cool. Isn't he adorable? I'm really psyched."

Catty went back to Chris, and Jimena turned back to Collin. He smiled sweetly, but even with the crush of kids dancing around them, Jimena felt too alone and isolated with him.

His hand was pulling her back to him when she caught Veto's face through the strobe lights. She almost ran to him. But something in the way Collin was touching her so tenderly made her hesitate.

She took in a deep breath and watched Veto walk toward her.

"You know him?" Collin asked from behind her.

She nodded. Veto looked incredibly sexy. His black hair gleamed in the flickering lights. His eyes were black and piercing. Every girl around her was staring at Veto as if he'd already broken her heart.

Veto stopped in front of her, took her hand, and pulled her away from Collin.

Collin was trying to smile, but Jimena could see the twitch in the corners of his mouth. It surprised her how much she cared about hurting him.

Veto put his arms around her and her worries slid away. He pressed her close against him and danced her slowly into a dark corner.

"None of the guys at Planet Bang are good enough for you, baby," he whispered into her ear. "They're all a bunch of wimps."

She laughed and smoothed her hands up his chest. She locked them behind his neck and gazed into his eyes. "All the guys are afraid of me," she confessed. "They never do more than look. But I know they like to look."

"The surfer's not afraid of you," Veto accused.

"Collin?" She glanced back. Collin was still staring at her. "Collin is my best friend's brother. He's like *mi hermano*. He just felt sorry for me, seeing me dancing by myself."

"*Chale.*" Veto looked back at Collin. "I see his eyes. I know what he's feeling for you."

She looked at Collin, then at Veto. Was Veto jealous of Collin? He had always been *celoso*. Jimena cuddled tight against him. "Don't worry about the surfer. *Tu eres mi todo.*"

She could feel Veto's lips against her ear. "I'm not worried," he whispered, and then his lips were trailing kisses across her cheek. She turned her lips to kiss him when Catty and Vanessa came up to them.

"Hey, Jimena," Catty squealed, pulling Chris behind her. "Introduce us to your friend."

"Yeah," Vanessa said. "Everyone is talking about him."

Veto seemed embarrassed.

"This is Veto," Jimena said.

Catty paled and Vanessa took a step backward.

"What's wrong?" Jimena asked, then she remembered. She whispered to Veto, "They think you're dead."

Veto laughed loudly. It was a hearty, full

laugh. "Do I look dead to you?"

Vanessa and Catty exchanged uneasy looks.

"There was a mistake." Jimena's words came out with a nervous twitter. How could she explain that a person who was dead *wasn't* dead any longer? "He's been alive all along. Just somewhere . . ." Her words trailed off. That was all she really knew. Veto hadn't told her where he had been.

Veto interrupted her and spoke with cool charm. "It's a long story, but basically, I had to fake my death. The casket was closed at the funeral and my family moved away right after for their own protection." He put his arm around Jimena and nuzzled her hair. "But I'm back now."

Vanessa and Catty seemed reassured, but Jimena wasn't. She had known Veto long enough to know when he was lying. A strange uneasiness filled her stomach.

Catty tilted her head quizzically. "You mean you were in something like the witness protection program?"

Veto grinned slyly. "Something like that."

"Cool," Catty said. "Wow. I want to hear all about it."

Jimena looked from Vanessa to Catty. It was easy for them to believe. And why not? Veto was standing before them obviously alive. But the small seed of doubt inside her was starting to grow. Where had he been?

Vanessa stepped back beside Michael. "We should celebrate after. Let's go to Jerry's."

"That's a celebration?" Catty rolled her eyes.

"I'm hungry," Vanessa clasped Michael's hand and started moving her feet. "We want pastrami sandwiches."

Catty shrugged. "All right."

"Sounds good to me," Chris said before Catty pulled him back to the dance floor.

Veto took Jimena's arm. "Come on. Let's get out of here."

"Don't you want to stay and dance?"

He shook his head. "I can't believe you're hanging out with such kids. They never would have been your friends before. They're the kind of people we used to laugh about." He seemed angry, but underneath the anger she understood his hurt and fear.

"You'll always be everything to me, Veto," she said when they were outside and she was sure he would be able to hear her over the music.

He studied her face to find the lie, but she stared at him and didn't shrink back. His face mellowed, as if he had suddenly become ashamed of his own jealousy.

He put his arm around her and nodded his head slowly, as if he understood that she had seen deep inside him and accepted his failings.

He glanced at the full moon. "Remember how you always liked the full moon?"

She glanced up at the sky. "Still do."

"Yeah, we spent a lot of nights sitting on your grandmother's fire escape staring up at the stars." He bent down and kissed her lips lightly, then whispered against her cheek. "Let's go someplace where we can be alone."

They walked away from Planet Bang and turned down a side street into a residential neighborhood. The fragrance of night jasmine wafted into the air and the purple blossoms from the jacaranda trees floated lazily around them.

"I didn't want to share you with the world tonight," he confessed. "It's been too long since I've been able to talk to you and I got a lot I need to tell you." He rested his arm on her shoulder.

They stepped across the street. Jimena was filled with dreamy anticipation, anxious for Veto to stop and kiss her.

Veto started to speak again, but something made him stop. She could feel his muscles tense. His eyes cautioned her and told her not to make a sound. He squinted into the darkness. A breeze tossed oleander branches back and forth and made dim moon shadows swirl across the lawn.

Veto eased away from the sidewalk to the side of a house, pulling Jimena with him, his movements furtive and silent. "Come on," he whispered. "We'll cut through the backyard to the alley."

She glanced at him. She didn't see fear in his eyes, only caution.

"You worried about enemy gangs?" His

alarm was making her uneasy. Veto had always been able to sense the presence of enemy gangsters and *la chota*. What was he sensing now? "We're not in anyone's territory. The neighborhood around Planet Bang is like City Walk. It's open to everyone."

He didn't answer her. He studied the layered shadows in the alley, then pushed her protectively behind him. "You don't know what lives in the night."

She started to answer *I do,* but a phantom shadow moved near the back of a garage and made her suddenly watchful. She strained to catch another glimpse of what she had just seen. Whatever it was seemed to have hopped to another shadow near an evergreen. The movement wasn't the frantic rhythm of wind rustling branches. It had been too solid and purposeful, like someone trying hard not to be seen.

She felt the need to protect Veto now and wondered what he would do if she told him the truth about who she was. Would he even believe her?

Veto took two steps toward the drooping branches of an evergreen, his feet crunching softly on the gravel, and froze again. "Did you hear that?"

"What?" her voice was low. She had only heard his footsteps. She looked down at her moon amulet. It was glowing. Now her body thrummed, wary and vigilant, as if something ominous were about to happen.

She touched Veto lightly. "We'd better go." She took a step backward and tried to pull him away.

"There," he whispered in a harsh, angry voice.

A figure formed in the shadows and slowly Stanton appeared before them, his dangerous eyes so blue they seemed luminescent.

Serena had told her that Stanton was a shape-changer; he could turn into a shadow and drift for miles, then reappear. She wondered if he also had the power of a vampire to shift into a bat or wolf.

She looked at Veto and her body filled with

new anxiety. Stanton's ghostly arrival hadn't startled him. Couldn't he sense the danger? Jimena tensed.

Stanton stood aside and Serena stepped from behind him. "That was way cool," she exclaimed in a happy voice.

Stanton's long fingers touched her lips tenderly and silenced her. "We have company."

Serena looked up and stopped short. "Jimena!" Serena walked over to them. "Introduce me to your friend."

"Yes," Stanton added, his voice as soft as the night. But there was something more in the way he spoke, as if he knew a secret. "Introduce us to your friend."

Jimena hesitated. "This is Veto."

"Veto?" Serena seemed alarmed. "I thought you were only teasing about Veto haunting you."

Jimena knew it had been a big mistake not to confide in Serena, but before she could offer an explanation, Stanton spoke. "Jimena also thought Veto was dead, but *voilà*—there he is as solid and warm as you or me."

Then he spoke directly to Veto, mockingly. "Everyone thought you were dead, Veto. What did you do?"

A cold knot tightened in Jimena's stomach. Why did Stanton seem to know Veto? And why wasn't Veto afraid of Stanton?

Stanton smiled, eyes fervent. "He's not afraid of me, Jimena, because he's a shade. Isn't that right, Veto?"

"Come on, Jimena." Veto grabbed her hand and tried to pull her away. "You want to waste the night listening to some *vato loco* who uses magic tricks to entertain his girl?"

Stanton laughed—a dangerous sound. It made Veto stop and look back.

"You don't want your girlfriend discovering the truth?" Stanton said. "I don't blame you. She probably wouldn't want to date a shade."

Serena looked at Stanton. "What's a shade?"

"A shade is like a ghost—"

Jimena interrupted him with a nervous laugh. "Veto isn't a ghost. He's no more dead than me or Serena."

"Of course, if he were only a shade he would feel as thin as vapor, but . . ." Stanton stared at Veto.

Veto didn't back down and he still didn't seem afraid. He held his head up and looked straight at Stanton in challenge.

Stanton continued. "Veto has been animated by the Atrox."

Serena looked at Jimena, then back at Stanton. "How can you say such a thing? That's not even funny. If he were animated by the Atrox, then he'd talk. The Atrox would know about you and me and send Regulators after us."

A derisive grin slowly spread across Stanton's face. He pushed back the blond hair that had fallen into his eyes. "He wouldn't, not Veto, because he doesn't even understand completely what has happened to him."

Veto didn't respond.

He's dead. Jimena could feel Stanton tickle the words across her mind. *And there's a part of you that has known the truth since you first saw him, but you wouldn't let yourself believe it.*

Jimena felt anger surge inside her. She turned and faced Serena. "How can you trust Stanton? Don't you know how risky it is to keep seeing him? He's an Immortal. What evil things did he do to get that status?"

Serena touched Stanton's arm. "He's changed."

"Changed? Maybe he's telling you he has, but he's also a master of lies and deceit. Can't you feel right now how he's feeding on the bad emotions between us?"

"I don't have any bad emotions toward you." Serena eyed Jimena curiously. "Why are you upset with me?"

"If you'd bother to get in my mind and read what I'm thinking, you'd know," Jimena said.

Stanton gently turned Serena's face to him. "Don't argue with your friend. She has to believe this on her own."

That was worse than if he had coaxed them to fight.

Stanton's slender fingers slid down Serena's neck and rested on her shoulder. They stared into each other's eyes. Jimena knew they were having a mental conversation.

Ugly emotions overwhelmed her. How could she be *tan celosa* of her best friend? She felt the jealousy take over. "I'm tired of covering for you and lying to Vanessa and Catty about your relationship with Stanton!" she yelled, immediately regretting that she had let her anger out. But instead of apologizing, she whirled around and started walking away.

Then another premonition hit her hard.

She lost her balance and fell to her knees as a picture swirled behind her eyes and came fiercely into focus. She saw Veto standing in MacArthur Park. She couldn't read the expression in his eyes. The earth ripped open behind him, exposing a bottomless pit, and Veto tumbled backward into the abyss. She watched helpless as he fell and the earth closed around him.

When the picture vanished, she looked up and saw Serena leaning over her.

"What did you see?" Serena asked with concern.

"I saw Veto." Jimena couldn't control the shaking in her hands. "I couldn't save him."

Serena looked around. "Where is he?"

Jimena turned her head. Veto was gone. Panic rose inside her. "I have to warn him! I don't want to lose him again."

Serena looked up at Stanton. "Jimena needs me. I'll see you tomorrow."

Stanton faded back into shadows and left.

The perfumed breeze blew across them, bringing the night jasmine with it. Stanton whispered a warning—"Be careful"—and his voice left a chill in the air.

CHAPTER TEN

THE DAUGHTERS MET at Serena's house. It was late and Jimena was still upset about her premonition.

Wally, Serena's pet raccoon, sat on the kitchen table. He stood up on his hind legs when Catty and Vanessa entered through the back door with a grocery bag. They sat down and opened a quart of chocolate ice cream. Catty took a spoon and dug in, then handed the carton to Vanessa, who dripped a long string of chocolate syrup into the carton.

"What's wrong with Jimena?" Catty asked.

"She had a premonition," Serena said. "About Veto." She didn't need to add that Jimena had never been able to stop her premonitions from coming true.

Jimena slowly told them what she had seen.

When she finished, Vanessa was the first to speak. "Maybe this premonition isn't as bad as it seems. Maybe Veto fell into a construction ditch and a rescue team pulls him out."

"Or maybe it was water," Catty put in. "Maybe he just falls into dark water that could look like a bottomless pit."

Jimena shook her head.

Serena shuffled her tarot cards. "Maybe Vanessa is right. There could be another meaning. Let's look at the cards and see if we get a clue."

Jimena hesitated. "I don't know."

"Let's try," Catty put her hand on the deck. "We'll all put our thoughts into it and see what comes out."

"Yeah, let's try." Vanessa tapped the deck with her knuckles, then dug her spoon into the ice cream.

"Okay," Jimena reluctantly agreed.

Serena shuffled the cards and set them in front of Jimena. Jimena picked one and handed it back to Serena.

Serena gasped. "The death card."

Vanessa dropped her spoon. It hit the table with a loud clatter.

"Yikes." Catty looked worried.

They were silent for a long time, each lost in her own thoughts.

Finally, Vanessa spoke softly. "The death card can mean the end of a relationship, right?"

Serena nodded.

Vanessa continued. "Then I think the card is for me. It's telling me my relationship with Michael is over."

They looked at Vanessa.

Vanessa bit her bottom lip. "I told him tonight that we should start seeing other people."

"But I thought you'd worked everything out?" Catty stared at her in disbelief.

"Yeah," Jimena added. "You were so cozy at Planet Bang."

Vanessa shrugged. "I know. I like him so much, but he's going on tour this summer."

"So?" Catty said.

"So . . . what kind of summer will that be for me? I mean, I like him and I know I'll miss him, but I can't allow myself to be defined only as Michael Saratoga's girlfriend. Besides he'll meet zillions of girls."

"You're crazy." Catty shook her head. "Michael is perfect for you."

Serena looked down at the table. "The death card can definitely mean the end of a relationship." Her words were so mournful that everyone stared at her. "The card isn't for you, Vanessa." Serena looked up and her words trailed away.

"Go ahead and tell them," Jimena urged. "They'll understand. You've kept it a secret too long."

"What?" Catty and Vanessa said together.

"I have a confession to make." It took Serena a long time to say the words. "I've been seeing Stanton, not just seeing him, but *seeing* him."

"*Seeing?*" Catty's eyes were wide with disbelief.

"As in, dating?" Vanessa couldn't hide the shock in her voice.

Serena nodded. "For a long time now we've been meeting secretly and . . . I really like him but—"

"But that kind of relationship is forbidden." Vanessa looked from Serena to Jimena. "You knew about this?"

Jimena nodded.

"And you didn't tell us?" Catty seemed angry. "You should have told us. Serena could have been putting us all in danger."

"It's just that I like him so much," Serena offered. "And he's different with me. He treats me nice. He's so sweet and—"

"What about the Regulators?" Vanessa asked.

"I know." Serena nervously clicked her tongue piercing against her teeth. "If I stop and think about the Regulators I get terrified because I know the Regulators would destroy us both. That's why I had to keep it a secret . . . from everyone."

"And how could the Atrox not know? Since it hasn't sent Regulators after you, aren't you concerned that Stanton's relationship with you is part of a bigger plan?" Catty asked. "Like Cassandra's plan?"

"I don't think so," Jimena defended her. "I've seen them together. I think he really cares about Serena."

"That time he trapped me in his memories," Vanessa started. "He didn't seem all bad. I actually felt sorry for him."

"Please," Catty interrupted. "This guy has tried to destroy us, and you're telling me you feel sorry for him?"

"I was deep in his consciousness," Vanessa argued. "And it just felt like part of him wanted to be free from his bondage to the Atrox."

A hush fell over them.

Finally, Jimena picked up the death card. "Maybe it's something else. Maybe the card is warning us about Cassandra. She's our immediate threat."

"You're right," Vanessa agreed.

"First thing in the morning we should go see Maggie," Serena added.

Jimena set the death card in the middle of the table and stared at the skeleton dressed in a knight's armor. End, transformation, change, and loss. Those were the words most commonly associated with the death card. She had heard Serena say them enough. None of those words boded well for their futures. She looked around the table and had a sudden feeling that they were all in inexplicable danger. It wasn't a premonition, exactly, but the odd feeling carried an inkling of foreboding that made her hands tremble.

CHAPTER ELEVEN

JIMENA PUSHED HER sleeping bag aside and waited for her eyes to adjust to the dimness in Serena's bedroom. Serena and Catty were sleeping on the floor at odd angles. Vanessa had fallen asleep on the bed.

Jimena wondered what had awakened her. If it had been a dream, she couldn't remember it now.

A clatter came from a distant part of the house.

"Veto," she whispered and stared out the bedroom at the dark hallway. Had he somehow followed her here?

The same sound came again. She was confident it had come from the kitchen.

She slowly stood and reached for her robe. Serena had rolled on top of it. Jimena gently pushed her off and pulled it out from under her. Then she crept into the hallway.

She tread softly over the carpet, her ears alert to any sound. When she reached the top of the stairwell, another thought came to her. Maybe it wasn't Veto who had made the sound, but Cassandra and Karyl. She took one slow step and then another until she was at the bottom of the staircase.

Her breathing sounded jagged and she wondered if her body had sensed some danger that her moon amulet hadn't picked up.

As she approached the kitchen she could hear the noises more clearly. The person wasn't trying to be quiet. Then she remembered Wally. She felt a sigh of relief. He had probably gotten into a cupboard and started digging through a bag of potato chips.

She pushed through the kitchen door.

Collin stood over the stove, bare-chested, wearing low-slung baggy sweats, his blond hair looking pale white against his darkly tanned back. He turned, and when he saw her, a broad smile crept across his lips.

"Hey, you couldn't sleep either?" He greeted her. "I'm making hot chocolate. Want some?"

She shrugged. "Might as well."

He pulled a bar stool from the center counter over to the stove and she climbed on top. Collin glanced at her bare legs, then quickly away. She shifted uncomfortably. She had spent the night with Serena many times and Collin had seen her in all kinds of strange pajamas, so why did she suddenly feel embarrassed now? He was like a brother to her. She pulled the robe closed more tightly.

Collin took more milk from the refrigerator and poured it into the pan.

"Did you have a bad dream?" she asked and watched his hand stir chocolate mix into the milk.

"The best dream and the worst dream." He chuckled.

"How's that?"

"I was surfing Jaws in Maui. The waves are so powerful you have to be towed by a Jet Ski to go fast enough to catch them." He took two cups from the cupboard. "It was the best dream. The waves were glassy and the ride was awesome. But then I looked up and saw this five-story wave towering above me. The peak broke over me and it became the worst dream. I couldn't breathe." He started stirring the milk again. "That's always when I wake up; right before I drown. I have to catch my breath just as if I'd been under the water. I don't go back to sleep after that."

"Sounds scary," she agreed.

He smiled at her. His eyes dropped and moved slowly over her body, then, as if he were embarrassed that she had caught him, he turned off the burner with a snap and poured cocoa into the cups.

Jimena started to take hers.

"Wait," he ordered.

She set her cup down.

"You have to have whipped cream and cocoa

sprinkles." He hurried to the refrigerator and came back shaking a canister of whipped cream. He turned it over and pressed his finger on the side of the nozzle, but only air came out.

"You're doing it wrong." Jimena took the canister. Her finger slipped and she sprayed two inches of whipped cream on Collin's chest. She burst out laughing.

"You did that on purpose." He didn't look upset, though. His eyes looked—Jimena stopped—what was that look in his half-closed eyes?

She wiped off the whipped cream with the tip of her finger and glanced up. Had he moved closer to her? She could feel the warmth radiating from his body.

"Jimena—" He started to say something, but his words fell away.

His hand rested on her shoulder and then he looked at her as if waiting for permission. Had her eyes said yes? His hand glided down her back, and closed around her waist.

She drew in a quick gasp of air, surprised

and intoxicated by the feel of his hand on the small of her back.

He leaned over her. Was he going to kiss her? She hadn't realized until that moment how much she had wanted him to. Her hands lightly caressed his arms, undecided and hesitating, but only for a moment, then they slid up to his shoulders and she became aware now of how close they were standing to each other. She enjoyed the delicious feel of his breath mingling with hers and parted her lips slightly in anticipation.

Then she remembered her premonition of the passionate kiss with Collin, and just as suddenly another premonition hit her with a horrific punch. She saw Veto tumbling into the bottomless pit.

She drew away quickly.

"Jimena? Are you all right?" Collin looked concerned.

"Yes," she snapped, and ran from the kitchen as if she were trying to run from the tumbling image of Veto.

"Jimena!" Collin called. She could hear his

bare feet padding on the floor after her.

He grabbed her before she reached the stair-well. "I'm sorry—" He started to apologize, but she jerked away from him and ran up the steps.

At the top of the stairs, she turned back and pretended not to see the hurt look on his face.

CHAPTER TWELVE

LATE SATURDAY AFTERNOON, Jimena walked up to the security panel and buzzed Maggie's apartment. Serena, Vanessa, and Catty waited impatiently behind her.

A metallic voice came over the intercom. "I've been expecting you." A loud hum opened the magnetic lock and Serena swung the door open.

Jimena followed everyone into the mirrored entrance. She glanced at her reflection. She had odd bluish circles under her eyes from not sleeping and her forehead was pinched in a frown.

"Come on." Catty held the elevator open for her.

Jimena jumped on. The metal doors closed and the elevator trundled up to the fourth floor.

"Why do you suppose Maggie said she'd been expecting us?" Vanessa asked. "Did one of you call her?"

Serena shook her head. "It means something's going on and she thought she'd see us before now."

"I bet it's about Cassandra," Catty guessed.

Vanessa sighed. "I knew we should have come to see Maggie sooner."

The elevator doors opened.

They walked down a narrow balcony that hung over a courtyard four stories below. Jimena plucked nervously at the ivy twining around the iron railing.

Maggie waited at the door to her apartment. She was a thin, short woman with long gray hair curled in a bun on top of her head. She hugged each of the girls and hurried them inside.

"So much has happened," Maggie murmured,

as she led them down a narrow hallway to a living room and kitchen. The windows were open and curtains billowed into the room.

Simple haunting music of four notes played from stringed instruments. Jimena looked around the tidy room. She had never been able to identify the source of the music. She knew it didn't come from a sound system because Maggie didn't believe in electricity. She thought it destroyed the magic in the night.

Maggie sat down. "So now, you're here about the thunder, correct?"

The girls shook their heads.

Maggie seemed surprised. "No? Surely, you've heard it?"

"We've all grown up with earthquakes," Vanessa offered.

Catty shrugged. "Yeah, it's not like an earthquake warning from Caltech is big news to us."

"Earthquakes?" Maggie seemed completely baffled. "You think earthquakes caused the sound?"

The girls nodded.

"We're here about Cassandra," Serena put in.

"Cassandra and Veto," Jimena added.

"Well, tell me then." Maggie looked at Jimena and waited. Her warm, caring eyes always gave Jimena the feeling that Maggie was inspecting her soul.

"Veto," Jimena began slowly. "I thought he was dead, but he isn't. I was so happy to see him again, but then I started having premonitions about him. In the first one I saw him with Cassandra. I'm not sure if she was reaching out to embrace him or to push him."

Maggie covered Jimena's hand with her own, encouraging her to continue. But before she could speak, Serena added, "Stanton saw Veto and said he was a shade."

"What's a shade?" Catty asked.

"It's very simple really," Maggie began. "The ancient Greeks believed that after death, the spirit keeps the same appearance it had during life so that relatives and friends who die after will be able to recognize it."

"You mean, a ghost?" Vanessa questioned.

"Not exactly. It's not the spirit of the person, but an airy ghostlike image of the person."

Jimena felt relief flow through her. "Veto's not a shade then. He didn't feel like empty air. I mean, I kissed him. He was warm and solid."

Maggie's hand clasped her arm tightly. "But . . ." she began.

"What?" Panic seized Jimena.

"If Stanton recognized Veto as a shade . . ." Maggie's words came out slowly, as if she were still considering what this could mean.

Jimena rushed for an explanation. "Stanton could have lied."

"If Stanton recognized him as a shade," Maggie continued, "then it could be that the Atrox animated Veto for some evil purpose. If so, then he would feel as real as any one of us."

Serena looked at Jimena. "Remember? Stanton said Veto had been animated by the Atrox."

Maggie nodded. "Veto's appearance could also explain the strange thunder I wanted to talk to you about."

"What about the thunder?" Jimena's heart was beating wildly. She rubbed her chest, trying to calm it.

"Land thunder," Maggie whispered and looked off to the side as if she were remembering something. "It's the sound Tartarus makes when it opens. I suspected that Tartarus was opening and if so, then that could mean that the Inner Circle was allowing someone of high importance to visit." Her eyes fell on Jimena again. "Or to escape."

"It's Cassandra," Vanessa whispered and looked to Serena. "Tell her what Stanton said."

"What about Cassandra?" Maggie asked Serena.

"Stanton said that Cassandra had suddenly gained favor with the Inner Circle, the Cincti he called it."

Maggie nodded. "Yes, the Cincti, those closest to the Atrox."

Serena went on. "Stanton said Cassandra had been allowed to visit the Cincti."

Maggie frowned slightly. "If this is true, it is very bad for us because it means that she has come up with an evil plan. And it must be a very good one for her to be allowed an audience with the Cincti."

"We'll stop her," Serena said confidently. "We've battled her before."

Catty twisted a strand of hair nervously. "Stanton also said that she had been given permission to go back in time and change one event."

Maggie didn't seem surprised. "That must have been part of her plan. But whatever she changed is already part of your past now. What worries me is that she must know something about one of you, something that could make one of you vulnerable. That vulnerability could put all of you in jeopardy."

Maggie became silent. She appeared deep in thought as she studied each of them.

"Tartarus," Jimena repeated the word slowly. She wondered if the name had filled the other Daughters with as much dread as she was feeling now.

Vanessa looked worried. "What is Tartarus anyway?"

Maggie's voice was solemn. "Tartarus is a dark abyss far below the surface of the earth."

A cold fear gripped Jimena's chest as she remembered her premonition of Veto falling. Was he falling into Tartarus? She shook her head, trying to rid herself of the picture.

"Tartarus is surrounded by a thick layer of night." Maggie glanced around the table. "It's a place of damnation where its residents suffer endless torments. Some say it is where the Atrox resides and, of course, we know that the Inner Circle meets there." She shook her head. "Someone being allowed to visit the Inner Circle, someone who is not even an Immortal. This is a big event."

Jimena clutched the table. She was afraid to let go for fear her trembling hands would reveal the depth of her concern. One desperate thought played through her mind. She had to find a way to keep Veto from falling into the bottomless pit. When she was finally able to speak, her voice felt shaky and the words tumbled out in a strange pitch. "I had a second premonition."

"Yes, dear," Maggie encouraged her to go on.

She waited a moment, taking deep breaths before she continued. "I saw the earth opening behind Veto. A huge bottomless pit. He fell backward. It seemed like forever, and then the earth closed over him."

Maggie began, "It is possible that Veto has been deceived by the Atrox and—"

"No, Veto is too smart for that," Jimena interrupted. "He wouldn't let anyone game him."

"The Atrox and its Followers can be very seductive," Maggie went on. "It's possible that Veto has been animated by the Atrox without even understanding what has happened to him. To be alive again—think of the joy he must feel if it is true . . . to be able to see you again."

An iciness shot through Jimena with a sudden shock. "Veto would never allow himself to be used that way!"

"Maybe he doesn't know," Maggie said. "And that what you saw in your second premonition was his return to Tartarus. The Atrox would demand it."

"Maybe he's part of Cassandra's plan," Serena suggested.

"Not Veto." Jimena could feel anger brimming in her chest. "How can any of you believe that about him? Besides, we're all basing it on things that Stanton has said and Stanton is an Immortal who owes his allegiance to the Atrox. So how can we believe him? If anyone is deceiving us, it's Stanton, not Veto. Stanton is probably part of Cassandra's plan and he's telling us lies to distract us from what is really happening."

Serena glanced at Maggie and blushed.

"That's possible," Maggie agreed. "But not probable. The sudden appearance of Veto at the same time as the land thunder leads me to believe Stanton."

Jimena took a deep breath, trying to control her anger. Why were Catty and Vanessa and Serena looking at her with such sadness? Had they already decided that Veto was a shade? She could tell from their faces that they felt sorry for her. That was worse than if they had been angry with her for protecting Veto.

She stood. Her legs felt wobbly. "Veto could never do anything that would harm me." She hated the way her voice sounded weak and rasping. "No one has given Veto a chance to speak. I'll ask him point-blank the next time I see him."

"But you must be careful," Maggie warned.

Serena looked up at Jimena. "If the Atrox has animated Veto, we'll help you find a way to free him."

"Of course we will," Vanessa added. "We're all here to help."

Jimena didn't want their sympathy. She glanced at her watch. "I got to go."

"Please stay," Maggie said.

"I have to go to Children's Hospital," Jimena answered. "I need to get my hours in or I'm in violation of a court order." She tried to control her voice when she spoke but she knew they heard the anxiety in her words.

"I'll go with you," Serena offered.

"No," Jimena answered, too quickly.

Serena looked at her oddly. Jimena hadn't meant for the word to come out so harshly. She hated the distress she saw in Serena's eyes.

"I need time alone to think."

Maggie nodded knowingly. "Come back tonight after you've had a chance to take all this in."

"Yeah," Serena said. "We'll wait here for you."

Vanessa and Catty nodded their agreement.

"Will you come back?" Maggie asked.

Jimena chewed her lip and nodded. "I will." But she couldn't look in Maggie's eyes. She knew that if she did, the warmth and concern she would see there would make her break down and cry.

She hurried outside to the balcony, down the fire stairs, and out into the afternoon. Tears shimmered in her eyes and she brushed them away with the heel of her palm before they could fall down her cheeks.

It couldn't be true. It wasn't true. Veto was innocent. But even as she was trying to deny it, another part of her mind was recalling Veto's strange appearance the first night she had seen him.

She ran down Robertson toward Beverly Boulevard, as if distance could somehow lessen the effect of Maggie's words.

Tartarus was another name for hell, and Jimena knew Veto didn't deserve to go to hell, no matter what bad things he might have done. He was good deep inside, and he never would have done the things he had if he hadn't had to take care of his younger brothers and his mother.

And then a thought came to her that made her slow her pace. Maybe it had been fear that had made them do those things. The thought grew inside her like a terrible weight. Perhaps they had acted so tough and violent because they were afraid that if they didn't, people wouldn't respect them. It was easy to be popular in the 'hood when you had a big reputation and everyone was afraid of you. What would their lives have been like if they had been regular kids? She stopped. Perhaps Veto would still be alive.

She turned the corner as the bus pulled away from the curb. Normally missing the bus wouldn't have bothered her, but this evening it felt like a terrible omen of what was to come. She looked at the eastern horizon. The moon hadn't risen yet, and the sky seemed empty and alien.

She paced back and forth behind the bus bench. This time the tears were stronger than her will to hold them back and she let them fall. She didn't know if she was crying for Veto or for herself.

If it were true that Veto had been animated by the Atrox, then did that mean she would eventually have to fight him? She didn't think she could. She wouldn't. She had to find a way to free him.

CHAPTER THIRTEEN

THREE HOURS LATER, Jimena finished her work at Children's Hospital and rode the bus home. Visiting with the children always had a calming effect on her. She could almost forget her problems when they smiled at her from their hospital beds and wheelchairs. She sighed and looked through the graffiti-scarred side window at the moon. She felt embarrassed for the way she had acted at Maggie's, but she was too tired to go back there. Tomorrow would be soon enough to apologize. Right now she wanted a warm shower and a long night's rest.

At last the bus passed Alvarado Street. She grabbed the handrail and walked to the front as the bus pulled to the curb. She jumped off and had started home when someone called her name.

She whirled around. Veto leaned against the metal beam supporting the weather shelter over the bus bench, his legs crossed in front of him, exactly the way he had waited for her only a year back.

"Hey, Jimena." His words were lazy, his look sultry.

She took two quick steps back to him and slapped his cheek.

A slow, steady smile crossed his face. "I guess things are back to normal."

"How did you get back to me, really?" she demanded.

His eyes looked confused, and he reached for her.

"You know what Stanton said about you?" she continued. "He said you were a shade." She studied his face for a reaction but the light on Alvarado had turned green, and now traffic was moving swiftly down Wilshire Boulevard. The car headlights rushed over Veto, and the whirling light made it impossible for her to read his face.

"Shade?" Veto shrugged, his lips frozen in a grin. "I'm Ninth Street. *Puro* Ninth Street."

"Not a gang!" she shouted. "A dead person."

His eyes seemed to quiver and she saw the slightest droop in the corner of his mouth, but those could have been illusions created by the headlights.

"Come on." He pulled on her arm. "Let's go over to Langer's for something to eat. I told you I wanted to explain everything to you."

He darted into the street, pulling her with him. They dodged traffic. Angry horns honked behind them. One car skidded to a stop as they jumped on the curb and ran across the grass into the park.

"Veto." She called his name sharply and he stopped. "You didn't answer my question."

"What?" He acted as if he didn't under-stand. He had learned to hide his emotions from years of being in a gang, but she knew him well enough to detect the slightest nuance. And without the interference from the car lights she read his face clearly. Her heart sank.

"It's true, then," she said sadly.

"What's true?" He put his arm around her. "You're letting your imagination run away from you. I told you I was going to explain everything to you, but you won't give me a chance."

She stared at him, not even blinking when she spoke. "Don't play any games with me. I need to know the truth."

A nearby homeless man tossed in his sleep and looked up at them through his stained pink blanket.

She pulled Veto away and they began walking toward the lake. The rain had started again, and Veto took off his jacket and put it protectively around Jimena's shoulders.

"I know what you've done." Her words came out in a whisper. "You let the Atrox animate you so you could come back. You don't understand what the Atrox is, and now I have to find a way to free you."

He walked quickly ahead of her, then turned back and punched his right hand into his left palm. "I'm proud of what I've done. Why can't you be proud of me? No one has ever dared to do what I've done for love. I tricked the Atrox so I could be with you again."

Jimena stopped. "Do you believe that?"

"The Atrox is no match for a homeboy from *el Nueve*."

"No one can trick the Atrox." Her anger matched his now and their voices echoed around them. "No one!"

"Why can't you believe me?"

"The Atrox is using you, Veto. There's too much you don't understand."

"It's you who doesn't understand." He held his face up to the rain as if it could cool his temper. When he spoke again his words were slow and sure. "Didn't I promise you that nothing was ever going to separate us? Not even death? I'm just keeping my promise to you. My homies always said that I could trick the devil. Even you used to laugh and say it was true. So I did." He turned away from the rain and looked at her. "I tricked the Atrox. I did."

Jimena knew he was telling the truth as he believed it, but was it even possible to trick the Atrox? "Veto, the Atrox is using you, and it's my fault because I'm . . ." Her words trailed off and she started again. "It's my fault the Atrox did this to you, because it wants to hurt me and my friends. I'll do everything I can to free you from its control."

He touched her arm. "Free me? *¿Por qué?* Feel glad for what I've done. I'm with you again, and you know with your heart that I'd never let anything bad happen to you. The Atrox can't hurt you with me around. I got your back."

She shook her head sadly. "The Atrox is probably going to use you to hurt me."

He chuckled. "If I were working for the Atrox and going to harm you, wouldn't I have done it already, before tonight, before you found out how I got here?"

He put his arm around her and pulled her close against him.

"I risked everything to be with you again," he whispered against her cheek. "I risked my soul."

A chill spread through her, and it wasn't from the rain drizzling down her back.

"Has any *vato* every done so much for love?" he continued, his voice caressing and convincing. "I did it for you, baby. For us."

"Veto." All the old ache and loneliness came back. "It was wrong what you did and dangerous. How am I going to save you?"

"You got the power."

She looked at him surprised. "You know about me? Who I am?"

"What about you?" He touched her moon amulet with the tip of his finger. "I'm talking about this. What are you talking about?" Veto lifted the amulet. Rain beaded on the moon etched into the silver.

Jimena breathed a sigh of relief. At least he couldn't be a Follower or even a danger to her. If he were, the amulet would have burned into his flesh. He balanced the amulet on the tips of his fingers.

"What about my moon amulet?" she asked.

"It can keep me alive without the animation of the Atrox," he explained.

Was that true? She believed in the power of the amulet, even though Maggie had tried to dissuade her. Maggie said the amulet was only a symbol of the power inside Jimena.

He played with the chain as if his fingers were searching for the clasp. "All you have to do is let me wear it."

"I never take it off." That's what she said, but she had the urge to take it off now and see what would happen. "Since you've been gone, Veto, I learned something about myself . . ." If she did tell him the truth, would it change anything? Or would he laugh and tell her she was tripping?

Veto interrupted her thoughts. "If you let me wear it, it breaks the spell of the Atrox and I stay alive."

"Why do you believe that?" she asked.

"Because . . ." He looked behind him to make sure no one was listening. She couldn't image what he was going to say now if the other things he had declared had not pushed him to caution. "An angel came to me the first night that I found a way to sneak out of the earth. She was beautiful and glowing. She told me to get your moon amulet."

Jimena wondered if it was the goddess who had come to her grandmother the night she was born.

"Yeah, *es verdad.* She helped me find clothes to wear . . ."

Jimena held her hand up, signaling him to be quiet so she could think. If the amulet was only a symbol, as Maggie said, then she supposed it would be all right to take it off and let Veto wear it. And maybe it had powers that Maggie didn't know about. Perhaps it could break the spell of the Atrox.

She pinched the amulet nervously.

"Come on. Just let me try it on for a minute to see what goes on. Then I'll take it off and give it back to you. What can happen? There's no one around here but homeless people and *tecatos. Vamos a ver.*"

She started to unclasp the amulet. As she

did, she remembered her grandmother's warning. The goddess had told her grandmother that Jimena would be safe as long as she wore the amulet.

When she fastened the chain around Veto's neck, the amulet began to glow, filling the dark around them with a peculiar white light. Almost immediately Jimena felt the intrusion of another mind in hers, and something more, a pain twisting inside her like currents of electricity.

She jerked around.

Cassandra stood behind her, eyes dilated, her features sharp as her face grimaced in total concentration.

Too late to defend herself, Jimena realized that Cassandra had been hiding nearby and was now in her mind, reaching into the depths of her being and ripping her power away.

Karyl stood beside Cassandra, but it was clear that she was acting on her own.

Jimena focused her powers and tried to block Cassandra from going deeper inside her mind, but it was too late.

She looked at Veto. "You betrayed me." The words took all her energy. The pain inside her was complete now. She fell, disoriented, to the wet asphalt path.

Cassandra and Karyl gathered around her.

"Goddess." Cassandra smirked.

"Destroy her now," Karyl whooped.

"Give me time to enjoy my victory." Cassandra beamed and walked full circle around Jimena, her heels tapping a staccato beat in the puddles. Her long black cape flapped around her and swirled over Jimena.

Finally, Cassandra stopped and took a deep breath. When she spoke, the satisfaction in her voice was high. "Finally it's done."

▼

CHAPTER FOURTEEN

"JIMENA." SHE HEARD someone calling to her from a great distance. Her eyelids fluttered and then her vision cleared. Veto was bent over her now, trying to protect her from the rain. She must have blacked out for a few minutes, because she didn't remember him kneeling next to her. She saw the intensity of the fear in his eyes and the hard set of his mouth and knew immediately that he hadn't betrayed her.

"I'll be all right," she muttered, but even that didn't ease the look in his eyes. Why was he so scared?

She tried to twist her head to see what was happening. Veto knelt closer to her and tried to keep her still. She glanced at him and when their eyes met, she knew. He was afraid of losing her.

Veto edged closer, eyes watchful. "What did she do to you?" he whispered.

"She took my power from me," Jimena answered.

"Power." Veto seemed confused. "What power?"

"My ability to see the future and fight the Followers."

"Followers?"

"People like Cassandra and Karyl," she answered. "They're Followers of the Atrox."

He seemed to understand.

"I told you." Her whisper felt hoarse. "The Atrox wants to destroy me. Since you've been gone I learned my true identity. I'm a goddess, a Daughter of the Moon."

Cassandra giggled behind her—a cold and evil sound. *"Were,"* Cassandra corrected her. "You once were a goddess, but no more. I took care of that."

Jimena saw the anguish in Veto's eyes. He understood now that he had been deceived. He started to unclasp the moon amulet that hung around his neck.

Cassandra stopped him. "Too late, Veto. It won't be any good to her now. You might as well keep it as a souvenir."

Karyl laughed. "Come on, destroy her!"

"Patience, Karyl," Cassandra murmured as if making the moment linger somehow made it better. "Besides, Morgan will want to see. Where is she?"

Veto tightened his grip on Jimena's arm. His eyes were staring at something across the park. "That's the angel I told you about. The one who helped me that first night."

Jimena turned her head. Morgan rushed down the asphalt path toward them, a spray of water splashing beneath her knee-high boots, her red mini wet and clinging.

Karyl snickered. "You did good, Morgan."

Morgan walked over to Veto. "You shouldn't believe everything a gorgeous girl tells you. Glitter makeup can make anyone glow."

That made Karyl and Cassandra laugh.

Then to Jimena she added, "Angel is such a natural role for me."

"Dark angel," Karyl corrected.

"My mind-control helped," Cassandra added. "It was easy to make Veto think he was seeing an angel."

Veto put on his stony *máscara* and held his head up and back. Jimena could feel his muscles tense. His hands formed into fists.

"Don't do anything," Jimena warned. "You don't understand what you're up against."

He stood. As he threw a fist at Karyl, thunder shattered the air. The ground around them shook and the earth ripped open behind Veto.

Veto balanced precariously on the edge of the precipice, his arms swinging wildly as he desperately struggled to keep from falling. Finally, he took a faltering step forward and smiled in relief.

Suddenly, Cassandra seemed to appear from nowhere. She walked quickly toward him and shoved his chest exactly as she had done in Jimena's first premonition. Veto lost his balance and as he started to fall backward, he turned with his last effort to face Jimena. His eyes held hers as he fell over the edge.

Jimena screamed, but the sound came out more a mournful groan. She dragged herself to the edge of the chasm and watched Veto tumble into the ink-black abyss, precisely as she had seen him fall in her premonition.

"Why did Tartarus open now?" Morgan's voice sounded worried.

"The Atrox must sense our success." Cassandra gloated. "And it wanted its puppet back."

Karyl's eyes fired with savage delight. "You think Veto will like it in Tartarus, Jimena?"

Jimena suppressed her tears and rose slowly, her legs barely able to support her. She took one halting step forward. Her voice was full of conviction when finally she spoke. "You haven't won, Cassandra."

Cassandra hesitated for only a second, her ice-blue eyes unsure, and then she laughed, the sound lifeless and pitiable.

"You're done, goddess." Cassandra's eyes began to dilate.

Jimena waited for her to strike, but Cassandra stopped and touched her temple as if she were feeling something strange. Jimena knew from the look on Cassandra's face that she was having a premonition.

When it was over, Cassandra smiled strangely. "This power stuff is a knockout."

"Did you see something?" Karyl asked.

"Yeah, wham, like a movie played behind my eyes." Cassandra's words rushed out in her excitement.

"Well." Morgan seemed impatient. "What?"

A satisfied look crossed Cassandra's face. "We defeat the Daughters in the biggest way."

Morgan whooped.

Jimena wondered what Cassandra had seen.

She listened carefully, hoping to hear a clue.

Karyl nudged Cassandra. "So tell us."

Cassandra started to walk away, smug. "I told you that if you steal the power from one of them, the rest will tumble."

"Yeah, like dominoes," Karyl agreed.

"My plan is working." Cassandra's pace quickened.

"Where are you going?" Karyl asked. "You're not going to get rid of her?"

"No, the premonition showed me a better plan," Cassandra said with alacrity.

Karyl seemed hesitant.

"I've seen the future, Karyl." She lifted her arms to the rainy night, and swirled suddenly around. Her black cape seemed to take flight. "Jimena is going to bring all the Daughters to the edge of Tartarus!"

Karyl smiled broadly.

"And I'll be part of the Inner Circle." Cassandra turned to leave, with Morgan and Karyn following close behind.

Jimena watched them go. She had never been

able to stop any of her premonitions from coming true. Did that mean she wouldn't be able to stop Cassandra's premonition from coming true either? She felt heartsick. Could all the Daughters be doomed because of her stupidity?

CHAPTER FIFTEEN

J

IMENA WAS BREATHLESS when she finally reached Maggie's apartment and pressed the security button.

"It's about time," Serena's voice came impatiently over the speaker. "Where have you been?"

Jimena tried to speak, but her throat was too dry to utter a sound.

"Jimena?" Serena sounded worried now. She must have sensed trouble, because the magnetic lock buzzed. Jimena opened the door and hurried inside.

Serena was waiting for her on the fourth-floor landing when the elevator doors slid open. "What happened?" Serena asked.

"Cassandra and Karyl . . ." Her words fell away when she saw the way Serena was looking at her. What did Serena see in her eyes? Could she tell just by looking at her that she no longer had her power of premonition? Or was it something else?

Serena put her arm around Jimena. "What did they do to you?"

Jimena couldn't find her voice.

"Come on," Serena helped her along the balcony. They entered the apartment as Maggie came back from the kitchen, carrying a tray with a tall glass of water. "Drink this, Jimena, and don't say a word until it is finished."

Maggie sat down and Jimena drank. She knew immediately it wasn't water, but a cold herbal mixture that tasted of sweetened barley. The liquid soothed her throat.

"Now, dear," Maggie began. "I assume from the way you look that your last premonition has come true."

Jimena nodded. "How can I go down to Tartarus and rescue Veto?"

Maggie studied her for a long time. "The way down to Tartarus is easy, but to retrace your steps back to the world above is impossible."

"I'm willing to try," Jimena pleaded.

"It's too dangerous." Maggie shook her head. "I cannot let you do it."

"I have to do something!" Jimena felt confused. She had thought Maggie would have a plan.

"I know you're concerned for Veto," Maggie spoke sternly, "but perhaps you should be more concerned with what has happened to you. I have warned you time and time again to be careful. If the Followers can stop one Daughter . . . eliminate her, then the power of all the Daughters is greatly weakened. Perhaps you should tell your friends what has happened."

Vanessa leaned forward with a nervous expression. Catty twisted a strand of hair between her fingers, her eyes expectant. Only Serena seemed to know already. She looked crushed.

"Cassandra stole my power," Jimena confessed. "I was careless."

"Tell them the full truth," Maggie coaxed.

"I took off my moon amulet and let Veto wear it." She hated the look of shock and sorrow on the faces of her friends. "But I know Veto is innocent. He was deceived, just as I was."

"Yes," Maggie agreed. "And now all your powers are weakened."

"Why don't we act now?" Serena suggested. "If we know where the Atrox is, then we should go now and strike first."

"Yes." Vanessa seemed suddenly animated. "Why do we always need to wait for the Followers to do something? Let's attack and get it over with. I hate all this waiting and anticipation."

Maggie shook her head slowly.

"Vanessa's right," Catty put in.

"We should be like a gang," Jimena added. "If you hear your enemy is gunning for you, then you strike first and hard."

Maggie sighed sadly. "I've told you. Daughters can never use the tools of evil to fight the Atrox."

Jimena finally voiced something that had worried her since Cassandra had taken her power. She spoke hesitantly, the other Daughters staring at her. "Without my power of premonition, am I still a Daughter of the Moon?"

Maggie hesitated too long. That was more answer than if she had voiced the words.

"Then I know what I have to do." Jimena stood and pushed back her chair.

"No!" Maggie cried sharply, as if she had read her mind and knew what Jimena was going to do. "Evil only feeds evil."

"You keep our hands tied," Jimena accused. The other Daughters watched her, amazed at her anger. "We should have done something before now. If you had let us act on our own a long time back, then maybe Cassandra wouldn't have been able to trick me and steal my power. Because we would have already destroyed her. Why do we have to act like monks?"

"You need a cup of tea," Maggie offered. "Something to settle your nerves. You're not the first Daughter that this has happened to, and you need to have a clear mind."

"I've had enough," Jimena said in a low voice. She could feel her body automatically assuming a threatening pose. She held her head back and looked at the others. "Are all of you going to sit around waiting for Cassandra's next move?" When they didn't answer, she continued. "Maggie knows nothing about fighting evil."

Serena looked away from her. Catty frowned and Vanessa seemed frightened.

"Leave it to a homegirl." Jimena stepped back. "I'll fight Cassandra and win."

She turned abruptly and started to leave.

"Jimena," Maggie called after her. "You mustn't do this!"

"But I'm not a Daughter anymore, am I?" Jimena asked. "Now that Cassandra has stolen my power. So it doesn't matter what I do, does it?" Her heart was racing. More than anything, she wanted Maggie to tell her what she had said wasn't true.

But Maggie only looked at her sadly.

▼

CHAPTER SIXTEEN

J

JIMENA WALKED WITH purposeful steps toward the door. Her hands trembled as she clutched the doorknob. No one called her back, not even her best friend, Serena, and that hurt. Was it so easy to let her go?

She yanked the door open, and then she was running down the balcony to the fire stairs. With each step she could feel the *locura* returning to her, that impossibly crazy-wild feeling she had had before when she was living *la vida loca*. Nothing could stop her. *Just do. Don't think.* She felt invincible again.

She hurried outside and started to run.

Someone called her name. She stopped and turned.

Collin jumped from his utility van. His hair was combed back in a ponytail, and he was wearing a Hawaiian shirt, baggies, and thick sandals.

"Hi." His smile was flirty and it annoyed her. "I'm waiting for Serena."

Sudden rage ripped through her. She resented that Collin's life had been so easy. It wasn't fair.

"Don't put your moves on me." Her voice sounded threatening.

Collin had been walking toward her and now he stopped abruptly. "What?" he asked with a baffled expression.

"You heard me. I know you're waiting for me and I don't have time to chat it up with some *gabacho* surfer. You go worry about your waves, pretty boy, I have things to take care of."

"What's your problem?" His words filled with anger of his own.

She looked at him thoughtfully. "You. That's my problem. Go find some perky girl who's all flirty and blue-eyed and doesn't understand what life is about."

Too late he tried to hide the startled look on his face.

She hurried away from him.

"Jimena!" This time when he called her name, she did not stop.

She had to figure out what she was going to do. She knew a gun wouldn't help against the Atrox, but a bullet would stop the Followers. Cassandra, Karyl, and Morgan weren't Immortals yet. A sly smile crept across her face. Wouldn't they be surprised to come face-to-face with her while she was holding a gun? Daughters had to live up to that goodie-goodie front and never use violence to fight the Atrox. But a homegirl . . . her fingers twitched, anxious for the heavy weight of a gun.

"You're going down, Cassandra," she whispered to the night. The need for revenge filled her heart and made her walk faster.

She could go to her homies. They would be happy to see her back and excited to go on a mission with her, but she didn't want to get them involved with the Atrox. She still felt as protective of them as she had in the years back when she was running wild with them and watching their backs. Maybe she could break into the gun shop on Alvarado Street . . . but that felt too close to home. She was sure someone would recognize her.

Then another idea came to her. She knew where to find guns. Lots of guns. In enemy land. It was dangerous, but it also felt like the perfect solution, and she liked the risk. Her heart started to race as it used to do before a mission. She could go to the abandoned house where she knew her old adversary, Wilshire 5, hid their guns and ammunition.

Forty-five minutes later Jimena hopped off a bus and hid in the dark shadows of a jacaranda tree as the bus pulled away from the curb.

She moved stealthily around the tree and scoped out the street. She knew where the Wilshire 5 liked to kick it. All she had to do was sneak past them in the shadows. Her heart found a faster rhythm, and she started forward. It had been a long time since she had gone on a mission. She liked the rush of adrenaline, the dry feel in her mouth, the hot nerves in her muscles. She wondered if this was the way the jaguar felt slinking around its jungle.

She had gone only a block when the solid beat of gangster rap boomed into the night. She clung closer to the shadows, eyes more watchful. A garage door was open and kids were dancing inside, knees locked together as they caught the beat and became one with the music. In front of the garage, silhouetted figures leaned against a wire fence, drinking forties and blowing cigarette smoke into the night air.

As she got closer she could see the *vatos* with their stubble-short hair and serious, alert eyes. The tattoos declared their allegiance to Wilshire 5. Some held 9-millimeter pistols. She wondered briefly how many times children had been caught in their crossfire. Had any of the kids she played with at Children's Hospital been shot by their stray bullets? She shook her head to erase the thought and glanced at the girls.

The girls had the same serious eyes as the guys, but most of them looked sad at the same time. They dressed in tight, low-slung jeans or too-short skirts and revealing Ts, advertising their sex, their *maquillaje* perfect and almost *payasa*. It made Jimena ill, the way some of the girls let the guys own them.

Only a few of the girls were warriors like Jimena. She recognized the hungry look in their eyes and the way they dressed differently from the other girls; in loose clothes so they could run fast, hit hard, and hide guns in their waistbands or taped to their legs. Those girls knew what a bullet could do to flesh and their eyes were as tense and watchful as the guys'.

Jimena hurried across the next street and let the shadows swallow her.

She passed a chain-link fence with razor wire curled around the top. A guy and girl leaned against the mesh, sharing secrets and kisses. She slipped around them and cut across an alley. She had only gone a short distance when she heard someone walking. The steps seemed furtive. She listened. The steps didn't continue. Maybe the night was playing tricks with her, but her gangster instinct told her she was being followed. Cautiously she slipped into the velvet blackness between a house and a garage and waited.

Finally she started again, eyes wary, looking around her.

She passed a long line of houses with boarded-up windows. Boxlike letters spray-painted on the walls warned the passerby to beware; they walked on Wilshire 5 territory. She slipped into the side yard, trampled through weeds, and hurried to the back of the old boarded-up house, then silently crossed the back porch.

She paused. Nerves tingled in her back. Long experience told her that someone was behind her. She held her breath and waited for a sound to give the person away.

At last, she decided it must be a dog or homeless person, and she brushed the wispy spiderwebs away from the door, turned the knob slowly, and walked inside. Wilshire 5 never kept the house locked. No one in their neighborhood would dare steal a gun from them. They never considered the possibility that someone from *el Nueve* would try such a dangerous thing.

A dank, moldy smell wafted up to her as she entered the deserted house. She listened intently for any sound. Wilshire 5 could come storming into the house at any moment. Some old grudge might suddenly be remembered after too many forties and send them for their guns, so they could go on a mission of revenge.

She stepped quickly, her footsteps pounding heavily on the wood floor. She reached the first closet. It was too dark inside to see, but already she could smell the bore cleaner and knew guns were hidden there and clean. She felt along the walls above the doorjamb until her fingers came across cold, chrome-plated steel. Her fingers worked quickly to take a gun off the nails. It was small and felt like a toy, probably some foreign special stolen from an old woman in a throw-down. She slipped the gun into her jeans pocket and felt in the dark for a heavier model.

A sound made her stop. Alert, she held her breath and listened.

Furtive footsteps stepped quietly across the floor. Whoever it was, he or she was trying hard to hide their approach. Had one of the kids at the party seen her? Or could it be Cassandra? Cassandra had stolen her power. Did that also mean that she now had some intuitive connection with Jimena and knew her whereabouts?

Jimena quickly removed the second gun. It felt heavy, hard, and cold in her hands. She liked the feel and was proud of the way she knew how to hold a gun. She was never going to kill a baby like some of these *vatos locos* who got a gun but never learned how to fire it. Working from memory, her fingers pulled the magazine from the gun. She held it in her hand, then, satisfied it was loaded, she slipped the full clip back inside. The metallic *click-clack* would alert the person on the other side of the door to her whereabouts, but she was ready.

Let them come, she thought, the jaguar in her smile. Her gun was loaded. She leaned back against the wall and waited.

The prowling footsteps stopped near the closet door.

Jimena made her wrists stiff and aimed the gun, even though she knew she was violating her probation and going against everything Maggie had taught her. Those rules no longer applied. She was the jaguar again and she was taking down the Atrox tonight.

She heard a hand brush against the door, then squeeze the doorknob. It turned slowly. She couldn't see it move in the dark but she could hear the soft ticking of metal as it turned.

She tensed and pulled back the trigger.

When the closet door opened, she fired.

CHAPTER SEVENTEEN

WHITE FIRE LICKED the ends of the barrel and a deafening explosion filled the closet. At the last second she had turned her wrist, and the recoil made the gun buck and hit her face.

"Collin?" His name wheezed from her lungs. She had expected Cassandra and Karyl, even some enemy gangster, but not Collin.

"Are you crazy?!" Collin shouted at her.

Pieces of plaster were still falling as Collin dropped to the floor beside her.

"Lucky for you I was able to twist the gun at the last second." Her head was throbbing from the recoil and her wrist felt like it was on fire.

"Lucky for me," he repeated in a thin voice.

Jimena took a deep breath. She was disgusted with herself. Maggie was right. Guns made violence too easy. How could she almost have gone back to *la vida*? Her hands worked automatically in the dark, taking the gun apart. The parts fell to the floor with dull, heavy thuds.

She shook her head. "You don't belong here, Collin. So why are you here?"

"No fear," he whispered.

"Yeah, right, no fear. Don't tell me you weren't afraid when I fired the gun, because I hate liars."

"Sure, I was terrified. But that's not the kind of fear I'm talking about."

"What is, then?" She tried to catch her breath.

His words seemed to resonate in the closet. "When you busted my act back in front of Maggie's apartment, I felt stupid for lying to you, saying I was there waiting for Serena. The truth is I had been hoping to see you, then when I lied to you and you rushed off, I realized I had lied because of fear."

"Fear?" she asked.

"Yeah, fear you'd tell me you liked me like a brother but didn't want to date me . . . you know the lines. I knew I had to find you and explain things to you."

"Explain what?" She was getting anxious to leave. The gunshot would have alerted Wilshire 5, and maybe even the cops. A police helicopter could be heading for them right now.

Collin continued. "I've liked you for a long time and that's why I've been following you around, going wherever I thought I could see you. Because I was afraid to just tell you the truth." He paused. "So?"

She didn't have time to consider her emotions right now. "So we got to get out of here before those *vatos* from Wilshire 5 come running to check out the gunfire." She stood.

Footsteps echoed hollowly across the floor.

"Too late," she whispered and cautioned Collin to stay down.

Karyl walked into the room, the bobbing beam of a flashlight in front of him. He shone the light in Jimena's eyes, then his light found Collin. Tymmie and Morgan came in after him, each holding a flashlight. They concentrated their beams on Jimena and Collin.

"Come with us," Karyl said flatly.

"You've got to be kidding," Collin answered.

"Do what he says and don't look in his eyes." Jimena grabbed Collin's hand and pulled him up. She didn't know what she was going to do. She had to protect Collin. There was no way she was going to let them turn him into a Follower.

Morgan stared contemptuously at Collin. She had had a huge crush on him once.

"Morgan, is this some kind of stupid high-school initiation?" Collin asked.

"This is dead serious." Jimena nudged him. "Just follow them."

"What kind of trouble are you in?" he muttered to Jimena.

"You wouldn't believe me even if I told you."

CHAPTER EIGHTEEN

KARYL AND TYMMIE walked them out to a battered Ford and pushed them into the back. The inside smelled of onions and old French fries. They stepped over McDonald's wrappers, and the remains of a Taco Bell burrito.

"What's going on?" Collin asked as Karyl slid into the driver's seat and turned the ignition. The tailpipes rumbled.

"No time to explain," Jimena whispered. "We've got to think of an escape."

Morgan crawled into the front next to Karyl. Tymmie pushed into the passenger's seat beside her.

Tymmie was tall, with white-blond hair and black roots. Three hoops pierced his nose and one pierced his lip. The hoops briefly caught a light from outside as he turned his head back to the front.

The car screeched away from the curb, and the sudden motion tumbled Jimena into Collin.

Morgan looked over her shoulder at Collin. The skin around the new piercing in her eyebrow no longer looked red. "I am so over you, Collin. I can't imagine why I ever liked you."

"Morgan," Collin answered. "Next time just send me a note, okay?"

Morgan's eyes narrowed to slits in anger. She didn't seem to like his answer, but she recovered quickly and smiled slyly. "No next time, Collin."

That made Karyl and Tymmie laugh.

Morgan turned back and Collin leaned closer to Jimena. "This is serious, isn't it?"

She nodded.

"We have to do something, then," Collin whispered. "If you're a victim of a crime and the criminal takes you to another location, you're probably not going to live."

"It might be worse than that," Jimena answered.

"Worse?" Collin looked totally confused.

Jimena sighed. "I guess there's a lot that Serena and I should have told you."

"Like what?" Collin asked.

Jimena looked into the rearview mirror and caught Karyl's smile, his eyes filled with desire. Then she remembered the second gun, the small one she had stuffed into her jeans pocket. Should she use it? Before she had time to consider what she should do, Collin nudged her. She looked at him.

"No fear," Collin whispered and glanced at the door handle.

Jimena understood immediately. Karyl was driving the car recklessly fast. He had already gone through one red light, blowing the car horn, and swerving around cross traffic, but he had to slow down sometime.

Jimena waited impatiently. Finally, the car started to slow at they approached a crowded intersection.

Jimena reached for Collin and held his hand, then opened the car door. Before Tymmie could grab them, they bailed.

They hit the pavement and skidded, scraping skin and jarring teeth. Cars swerved to avoid hitting them. Jimena could feel the heat of the car engines as they raced around her. She sat up, dazed, and looked at Collin.

Blood trickled from the corner of his mouth. He wiped at it with his tongue.

"No fear," he mouthed, and his eyes seemed lit with fire. "Now you know what a wipeout feels like."

She looked back at him with a wicked smile. "Now you know what living the life feels like."

"You're crazy," Collin told her, but she knew he meant it as a compliment.

"I know," she answered. "So are you."

"Yeah," he said with pride.

The Ford screeched to a stop and started backing up. Burning rubber smoked from the tires. The passenger-side door opened, and

Tymmie had one leg out, ready to jump after them.

"Come on," Collin yelled and took Jimena's hand. They dove into a yard, climbed over a fence, and ran across a backyard.

She could hear Karyl barking orders to Morgan and Tymmie. "Cassandra wants her now!" he yelled. His words echoed into the night and then slowly faded.

Finally, Jimena felt safe enough to slow their pace. They walked the rest of the way to Collin's van. Collin kept pinching his nose and checking for blood.

She looked at Collin with new admiration. Was she falling for him?

"So what were the things you should have been telling me?" he asked finally.

She bit the side of her cheek. Should she tell him? Would he even believe her?

"You remember that night Serena and I came home and told you we were goddesses and you thought we were teasing?"

His head jerked around and he studied her.

"Are you trying to tell me you weren't teasing?"

"Well, that's kinda true."

He started to smile and stopped. His eyes widened only slightly, and she knew he was ready to hear the truth.

CHAPTER NINETEEN

B Y THE TIME THEY reached his van, the street was deserted and a calm had settled over the night. Collin opened the passenger-side door and waited for her to climb in.

Jimena hesitated. "I've got some things I have to do still."

He nodded and slammed the car door. She walked with him to the driver's side.

"One more thing." Jimena touched his hand lightly. "Let me talk to Serena before you tell her you know."

He opened the car door and climbed behind

the steering wheel. "Are you sure you don't want me to stay and help?" She shook her head and was grateful when he didn't try to convince her to let him stay. He turned the ignition and she watched him drive away.

She wasn't concerned that she had told Collin about the Daughters of the Moon. It didn't really matter now that he knew her true identity, because she didn't think she would survive the night. And if Serena didn't want Collin to know, she simply had to enter his mind and hide Jimena's confession behind old memories so he wouldn't be able to remember what Jimena had told him.

Jimena walked down the street to MacArthur Park. The hour was so late that even drug dealers had deserted the park. Jimena circled the lake, listening for the land thunder and searching for a possible entrance to Tartarus. Then she slipped silently into the shadows and waited.

She leaned against a tree trunk. The wind blew, scattering the leaves overhead and revealing the cold face of the moon. Jimena looked up and a simple prayer spilled from her lips, *"O Mater Luna, Regina nocis, adiuvo me nunc."* Normally the prayer was only said in times of grave danger, but this felt worse to her. She would gladly face any danger, but she couldn't allow Veto to spend eternity in the tortures of Tartarus because of her stupidity.

"Please," she whispered.

She heard something behind her and turned without making a sound. A glow filled the darker shadows. A woman stepped toward her, walking three large slender dogs. The beam from her keychain flashlight ran swiftly over the grass and then across Jimena's leg.

The woman stopped in front of Jimena. Her dogs balanced on their hind legs, straining against their leashes as if ready to pounce.

The woman flicked off the light. Her hair was as black as midnight and flowed down her back. Her face seemed lit with the moon's radiance. A semicircular piece of white cloth was draped softly around her body and she wore sandals. She had a conspiratory grin. "Out rather late, aren't we?"

Jimena shrugged and stared at the lake. She didn't need conversation with a lonely woman tonight.

"Why are you in the park so late tonight?" The woman was trying to be friendly.

"I'm waiting for the earth to open," Jimena said matter-of-factly. Maybe if the woman thought she was crazy or high on drugs she'd go away and leave her alone.

But the woman looked her straight in the eye. "You want to go to the house of death."

A chill passed through Jimena. She had a strange feeling that the woman wasn't who she seemed to be. She was either Maggie in one of her many disguises or maybe even the goddess who had helped her grandmother the night she was born. "Is your name Diana?" Jimena whispered at last.

"Have we met?" the woman asked, and leaned against the tree next to Jimena.

"You helped my mother the night I was

born," Jimena said breathlessly.

"Do I look that old to you?" The woman restrained her dogs. They whimpered impatiently, finally circled and lay beside her.

Jimena shook her head slowly. She had never seen a woman look so lovely.

"And how do you plan on appeasing the spirits of the dead if you do go to the land of the dead?"

Jimena looked at her strangely. Was she serious? "What do you mean?"

"You're going to their house. What do you have to offer them so they will let you leave?"

Jimena thought a long moment. What could the dead possibly want from her? And then she remembered her grandmother's *oraciones* for her grandfather. "My prayers."

"Prayers?" Jimena could sense the woman's disappointment. "I remember a time when blood sacrifice was made. People slaughtered the pride of their herds."

"I don't have any cattle or sheep," Jimena offered. "I live in the city."

The woman snorted. "No one really believes in the mythical world anymore. Once people poured libations for the dead."

"Libations?"

"Milk and honey, mellow wine, and water sprinkled with glistening barley. Prayers? Well, I guess that is a modern equivalent. I suppose prayers will have to do."

"I could say them in church every day for a year," Jimena promised.

The woman considered that, then very carefully she spoke. "No one has ever been able to rescue a loved one from the world below." The woman looked up at the night sky. "Orpheus tried."

"Tell me," Jimena urged.

"Beloved Orpheus went to the underworld to rescue his wife after she died from a snakebite. Hades and Persephone agreed to let his wife leave because Orpheus had shown such proof of his love, but they set a condition. He was to return to the world of the sun without looking back at his lovely wife during the entire journey."

"And?"

"Eager to kiss his wife and afraid that she might not still be there, he looked back, and right before his eyes she died a second time."

Jimena considered the story. "I can do better. I will." She turned to the woman, hoping to convince her. "I only need someone to show me the way down."

The woman nodded sadly.

Thunder quaked through the ground, jolting through her bones. Jimena felt her heart race.

A soft lapping sound made her look across the lake. An old homeless man poled one of the boats toward her.

Jimena followed the woman to the asphalt path. The dogs strained against their leashes.

The woman gave Jimena a sorrowful look. "Every day you'll pray?"

Jimena nodded.

Finally the boat reached the lakeside and stopped. The old man had fierce eyes that seemed lit with a passionate fire. Filthy clothes hung shapeless on his skeletal frame, and he smelled foul. Jimena wondered how long it had been since he had washed his knotted hair and beard.

"Step into the boat," the woman said.

Jimena would have refused, but then she remembered the odd way she had seen Cassandra step onto the paddleboat. She raised her foot.

"Stop there," the man cried.

She paused.

"Tell me why you've come," he ordered. "It breaks the law of the gods for my Stygian craft to carry a living person."

"Nonsense!" the woman huffed, and handed him a gleaming coin. "I say she goes."

He took the coin with gnarled, dirt-caked hands and stuffed it into his clothing.

The woman nudged Jimena forward. She stepped onto the boat, almost losing her balance, then dropped into the seat, rocking the boat violently. The man balanced himself on the nose covering the bow until the paddleboat was steady again.

"*Quae tibi nocere possunt, etiam te adiuvare possunt,*" the woman said.

"What?" Jimena turned back, but the woman and her dogs had already disappeared.

She repeated the words. *"Quae tibi nocere possunt, etiam te adiuvare possunt."* She thought a moment. "What can harm you, can also help you."

The old man grimaced and poled the boat toward a rolling mist that had gathered on the water. Jimena heard cascading water and wondered if the fountain in the middle of the lake could possibly make that much noise.

They entered the mist and suddenly the earth opened before them.

The old man grinned at her. "This is the river over which no soul returns."

They plummeted down a waterfall into darkness.

CHAPTER TWENTY

THE BOAT SETTLED at the bottom of the waterfall and headed forward into a wide-mouthed cavern. The air became sulfurous and thick and impossible to breathe. The churning waters turned opaque with mud, then still and dead.

Whispering cries surrounded Jimena, and she could feel something in the dark touching her like wispy cobwebs. In the distance dogs were barking constantly. When her eyes adjusted to the dusky light, she realized it was the ghostly forms of shades who were touching her, their sad faces begging her for release.

The man poled the boat toward shore and signaled for her to step off. Her foot slipped as she stepped into gray-green moss. As soon as she was on shore, countless drifting shades surged around her. She supposed she was in Tartarus now.

She recognized Veto's dim form in the dark. He looked angry. He floated to her. "Why did you come?" His voice was no more than a dry whisper.

"I couldn't let you stay here," she answered. Now that she was here, she wondered how she was going to free him.

"Go back," he ordered. "Save yourself."

"I won't go. I'll stay unless you go with me."

Then she felt a coldness and saw silken black shadows moving toward her.

"Is that the Atrox?" she asked warily.

"It's a spirit from the Cincti," Veto whispered, as the frenzied shadow pushed through the shades, then charged, twisting with tumultuous fury and howling. Jimena struggled to stand against the force, then froze. Terror tried to rise up inside her and push her to move, but a strange torpor had taken hold. It had been a crazy idea for her to come down here. She felt doomed. Why continue to struggle? Give up. Make it easy. Was she thinking those words, or were they being put into her mind? It didn't matter. She surrendered.

Veto tried to grab her, but his touch was more like a rustling of air. "What are you doing?" His voice had faded to a dry hissing noise.

A sweet lethargy had taken over and she didn't answer him. She wanted more than anything to sleep. She lay down on the dirt as an abnormally dark shadow eclipsed the others. It seeped into her lungs with complete coldness. She let it in and felt herself drifting in a lazy way.

Veto stripped the moon amulet from around his neck. "Save yourself," he tried to yell but his words were barely audible. "Leave."

She shook her head.

He clasped the amulet around her neck.

"It's only a symbol," she said in a drowsy kind of way. "Only a symbol of the power inside me."

"Then feel that power," Veto urged.

She glanced at him. It was too late.

But as she continued to stare into Veto's fading eyes something happened. She realized instinctively that the real power had always been inside her. It was something no one could steal from her. She could feel her energy building, pulsing through her like a jaguar in the night. Her gift of premonition and the amulet were only symbols. She understood now that Maggie had wanted her to realize this for herself; she had never stopped being a Daughter of the Moon. If Maggie had simply told her that she had the ability to stand against evil without using violence, or her gift, then she never would have found the self-confidence and faith that she felt rising in her now. She gasped for air, then coughed and spit.

The shadow whipped angrily about her. She stood and concentrated all her power on forcing the phantom creature out of her lungs and away.

"Go," Veto told her.

"I can't leave without you," she answered. "I won't."

She pushed his dim form forward. The shadows swirled and gathered force and chased after them.

Above them she heard rumbling. Was that the earth closing over them, or opening to release them from the land of the dead?

CHAPTER TWENTY-ONE

THE SHADOWS THAT had chased after Jimena and Veto with such fury stopped suddenly. The following silence was more terrifying. It hung heavily around them with the promise of something worse to come.

Jimena glanced up. Overhead she could see the crack in the earth's crust.

"The rumbling must have been the earth opening," Veto said.

Jimena felt hope rising, but just as suddenly her optimism vanished. Maybe the Atrox had opened the earth to allow them to escape because there was more to its plan.

They continued up a narrow path through rocky terrain covered with silt and sliding mud. The soft glow of moonlight shining through the rip in the earth illuminated Veto's ghostly image. He seemed to float more than climb as he led the way up.

Then they heard a crash of thunder.

Jimena looked up. The earth closed over them. All hope was lost. In the pitch-black darkness that followed, Jimena tried to climb forward but she lost her grip and slid down over craggy outcroppings, ripping her palms. Finally, she caught herself on a slab of stone. She waited in complete darkness, trying to capture her breath.

"Don't worry," Veto whispered beside her.

She hadn't even been aware that he was with her until he spoke.

"I'll show you how I've been sneaking out of Tartarus to see you." His words sounded sure.

He started forward again, up through a cramped cavern. It was dark and misty inside. A pale greenish light seemed to emanate from the churning mists. Jimena crawled after him. She kept imagining movement in the darkness around her. Something brushed against her cheek and then was gone.

A terrifying shriek filled the passageway.

She stopped, her heart slamming against her rib cage. The cries sounded like three dogs howling in terrible distress. Their wailings pierced her ears and filled her with an uncanny fear. She had never been afraid of dogs before.

"What is it?" she asked Veto, her voice shaky.

"A dog guards the entrance," Veto explained.

"That's only one dog?" she asked and started to turn her head.

"Don't look back," he cautioned. "You don't want to see."

She didn't look back. She didn't want to know what kind of dog could make such a terrifying sound.

A few minutes later, they crawled from the narrow passageway and stood.

"Careful now." He led her along the thin and

crumbling bank of a vast underground river.

Veto's body seemed more dense now. He took her hand to guide her, but his flesh felt too soft and she had the strange feeling that if she grasped his hand too tightly she would press completely through it.

They edged along the bank. Mud and dirt gave way beneath their footsteps and fell into the water below.

The murmuring flow of the underground river was starting to make Jimena drowsy. She pulled away from Veto, cupped her hands and scooped them into the water.

Veto pulled her up and away. "What are you doing?"

"I was getting sleepy," Jimena answered. "I thought some water would wake me up."

"Not here." Veto nudged her forward. "The souls of the dead drink these waters to forget their lives on earth."

She stared down at the water, her tongue dry and her desire to lap the waters huge.

A channel of gray light struck her eyes. She

squinted. She was sure it wasn't an illusion, but light from the outside.

"Stay here," Veto ordered. He pulled himself up. Dirt spattered down on her, then his hand reached for her. She took it. His skin felt warm and solid now.

She scrambled out after him, surprised to find herself standing in the middle of MacArthur Park. Traffic moved slowly down the wet streets surrounding the park, headlights reflecting off the pavement. She gratefully held her face up to the rain and let it wash the dirt from her face.

"See, easy." Veto smiled triumphantly.

"Too easy." She shook her head sadly.

His smile fell.

"Our escape was too easy," she warned him. "It has to be part of some larger plan." She sensed that the Atrox was still planning to use Veto to destroy her. They stood in the rain, trembling and unsure.

"If it's still planning to use me," Veto said, "then let's show it that it can't. Risk it all, Jimena. The Atrox hasn't won yet."

She clasped her moon amulet, thinking. There had to be a way to free Veto from the Atrox, but how?

"We need to find someplace safe." She grabbed Veto's hand and pulled him.

"What?" He followed after her. "Where are we going?"

"We have to hide," she answered.

They ran across the park, sloshing through rain-soaked grass. She thought of heading to Maggie's. Maybe she would know how to protect Veto, but that journey required the use of a bus and she felt intuitively that they didn't have that kind of time.

"There," she said suddenly and pointed to a church.

Veto rushed ahead of her up the wide steps and reached for the door. When his fingers touched the metal handle, a bluish flash of lightning struck his hand and he tumbled backward.

Jimena understood at once. Veto was denied entrance into the church because he was still animated by the Atrox, the primal source of evil.

"Go inside. Protect yourself," Veto ordered.

Jimena dropped to the ground beside him. "I can't abandon you."

The air around them changed. The rain stopped suddenly, and she knew the Atrox was coming.

CHAPTER TWENTY-TWO

AN OVERWHELMING CALM filled the air.

Jimena looked around her, expectant, knowing the Atrox was about to attack.

Then a strange sureness came over her and for the first time since Veto had returned to her, she knew what she had to do. She stood and opened the church door. Holding it propped against her foot, she reached for Veto. "Come on."

"I can't go inside." His eyes looked with

to be controlling him now. He started to walk down the wide steps that led up to the church, his eyes staring back at her with pure hate.

She was filled with utter and complete despair. She couldn't bear to lose Veto this way.

"No fear," she whispered. The wind ripped the words from her lips but not the power she could feel building inside her.

She battled against the wind to open the door, using her body as a wedge to force the door against the building. When she had it propped open, she charged down the steps to Veto, grabbed his hand and propelled him inside.

A tortured scream left his body as he stumbled over the threshold.

The wind slammed the door behind them.

Immediately Veto began to weaken and fade, but he didn't seem afraid any longer. He looked peaceful and happy.

She helped him sit on a back pew.

"I promised you nothing was ever going to separate us," Veto said softly, his words only whispers. "Not even death. I tried, Jimena."

longing into the interior of the church.

"Yes, you can. Part of you is still Veto." She motioned with her head. "Hurry. The Atrox can't reach you there."

He stood up tentatively as if a great weight pressed down on him. He bit his full lips in a grimace when he tried to take a step forward.

"Hurry!" She could feel an unnatural storm building around them.

Without warning a gust of wind ripped the door from her hands and screeched around her in wild triumph. The door banged closed and she staggered backward.

Veto's face was a mask of fear.

She struggled against the wind. This time it took all of her strength to move the heavy wooden door.

"Go inside!" she yelled, but she doubted Veto could hear her. His eyes seemed touched with something unfamiliar.

Wind hammered down on her in cold gusts. She could feel her strength ebbing. She felt afraid, not for herself, but for Veto. A huge force seemed

"I know." She knew that she was watching him die a second time.

"I'm fading—I can feel it," he explained.

"It's going to be okay." She touched him reassuringly and wondered what emotions he must be feeling.

"I'm scared," he started again in a low voice. "It's from loving you so much and not wanting to lose you."

"Don't be afraid, Veto." she cradled him in her arms. "You won't be alone. Part of me is going with you. That's how it feels anyway. Part of me will always belong to you."

He smiled but it seemed to take all of his strength. "Go light a candle for me. Pray to *La Morena* to beg God to take back his fallen angel."

Afraid that he might slip away before she had one last look at him, she hesitated, then bent down to kiss his cheek. It was like kissing air. His hand reached for hers but was unable to clasp it.

"I'll light the candle." She started to go to the sanctuary, but Veto stopped her.

"Go with that punk *gabacho*," Veto said. "He'll love you fine."

Unable to speak, she nodded, but she didn't think she could ever love someone again.

She stepped slowly to the sanctuary, took a wooden match from a tin container and lit a small white candle. The flame flared as she felt, more than heard, Veto speak to her. "I'll always be with you."

She was afraid to turn back and see what she knew was true. When she finally did, he was gone. She walked to the back of the church and sat on the pew, still warm from Veto's body.

When the flood of tears finally subsided, she remembered what the woman in the park had told her. *"Quae tibi nocere possunt, etiam te adiuvare possunt."* She thought a moment. "What can harm you, can also help you." And she made a decision.

She wiped her face on her sleeves, then stood to leave, but stopped abruptly. The rain beating against the stained-glass windows didn't sound like the workings of a normal storm. She hadn't noticed the way the wind screeched around the roof while she was crying, but now she did. The storm seemed malevolent and alive and waiting for her.

She decided to spend what remained of the night in the church. She stretched out on a pew, ignoring the angry sounds of thunder that seemed to shake the very foundation of the small church, and soon fell asleep.

When she woke up, soft gray light filled the sanctuary and rain was gently tapping against the stained-glass windows.

She stepped outside. Soft rain sprinkled her face. She started walking back to her grandmother's apartment. She had only gone a little way when she saw Serena running toward her, a red umbrella sheltering her from the rain.

Serena ran up to her and held the umbrella protectively over Jimena. "I've been waiting at your apartment all night. I'd just about given up hope. Collin came home—"

"I told him."

"I know. I was so worried about you. I knew you were going to try to go down to Tartarus to rescue Veto."

"I did."

"I would have gone with you," Serena told her.

"Thanks," Jimena answered. "But it was something I needed to do alone."

"Come on." Serena started walking quickly toward the bus stop. "Catty and Vanessa have been looking for you, too. We're meeting back at my house."

Jimena followed after her.

CHAPTER TWENTY-THREE

B Y THE TIME JIMENA had finished shower-
ing and blow-drying her hair at Serena's house,
Catty and Vanessa had arrived. They looked up
when she entered the kitchen, then ran to her and
hugged her.

Even Wally, Serena's pet raccoon, seemed
happy to see her. He climbed off the table and
scuttled flat-footed over to her and stood in a
begging posture.

"Don't ever do that again," Catty warned. "You can't go off without us."

"That's right," Vanessa added and offered Jimena a cup of hot cocoa. "We're a team."

Jimena sipped the sweet chocolate. It tasted like the best she had ever had.

"Well," Catty asked impatiently. "Did you go down to Tartarus?"

Jimena nodded.

Serena sat down next to her, holding Wally on her lap.

After Jimena told them what had happened, she carefully explained her plan to take her gift back from Cassandra. When she finished she looked around the table.

Catty nervously pulled at a strand of hair. "It's risky, especially if Cassandra is anticipating your plan."

"How could she be?" Jimena asked.

"She stole your gift. Maybe the two of you have some kind of intuitive connection now."

Jimena nodded. She had already considered this. "If we did, then I think she would have been waiting for me in the park when Veto and I escaped."

"All right then." Catty seemed satisfied.

Vanessa bit her lip. "I don't know if I have enough power to keep both Serena and Catty invisible for so much time. I've only made Catty invisible before, and I didn't have much luck with that."

"You'll have to try," Serena said. "That's the best any of us can do."

Serena set Wally on the floor. "We really don't have a choice. It's the only plan we have."

Jimena studied her friends and hoped that her plan didn't fail. She remembered Cassandra's words. Cassandra had told Karyl that she had seen Jimena bringing all of the Daughters to the edge of Tartarus.

Jimena shuddered. She had to make sure that they met Cassandra as far away from the park as possible.

CHAPTER TWENTY-FOUR

THE NEXT DAY Jimena cut classes again and spent the afternoon looking for Morgan in Hollywood. Low-hanging clouds misted over the Hollywood sign and the day grew steadily colder. She knew Morgan didn't have enough power yet to be able to read her mind and discover her plan, but she was confident that Morgan could set up a meeting for her with Cassandra.

Finally, she found Morgan strutting past the Egyptian Theatre, holding an umbrella, her shiny black boots splashing in the puddles.

"Morgan!" Jimena called.

Morgan turned sharply. Jimena wasn't sure if it was a look of fear or disgust that crossed her face.

"I need your help." Jimena walked toward her.

Morgan took a step backward, unsure. "What do you want from me?"

Jimena tried to act humble. "I want you to persuade Cassandra to meet me tonight in front of the Pantages Theatre."

"Why?" Morgan's eyes narrowed suspiciously and her fingers touched the gold hoop pinched through the skin around her eyebrow as if it still felt tender.

"I want to talk to her about getting my power back." Jimena tried to make her voice as sincere as possible.

"*Your* power? It belongs to Cassandra now." Morgan smiled shrewdly. "But if you really want to see her, she'll meet you tonight in MacArthur Park."

Jimena felt her heart race. She didn't want the meeting to take place anywhere near the entrance to Tartarus. "Let's meet here in Hollywood," she suggested.

Morgan twirled her umbrella nervously. "You only live a few blocks from the park." She tilted her head coyly. "Why would you want to meet here?"

Jimena didn't have an answer. "All right. The park, then."

Morgan seemed too happy with her response. "Tonight in the park," she repeated. "Be there."

As Jimena watched Morgan walk away, a new worry took hold. Instead of trapping Cassandra in *her* plan, she wondered if Cassandra had now trapped Jimena in a plan of her own.

Back at the apartment, Jimena called each of her friends and told them to meet in the park tonight.

Then she went to her grandmother's bedroom and unlocked the trunk that sat at the foot of the bed. She lifted the lid, and the smell of mothballs filled the air around her. She dug through the clothes packed in the trunk until she found the blue halter top and black jeans she had been wearing the night Veto died. She wasn't sure why she had saved them, but she was glad she had, now. She was going to wear them tonight in honor of Veto.

She carried them back to her room, stood in front of the mirror over her dresser, and slipped on the gold earrings that had been a gift from Veto. Then she started to dress. She rubbed glitter lotion over her arms and painted black lines on her eyelids. She rolled on mascara, then stood back.

She studied her reflection. There was one last thing she needed. She wasn't sure there was enough time, but she knew she wasn't going to the park until it was done. She couldn't do it by herself, but she was sure Catty could help her.

She started to leave her grandmother's apartment but stopped at the door, remembering the smaller of the two guns she had stolen from Wilshire 5. She hesitated. She knew it was wrong, but it might also be the only way she could save Serena, Catty, and Vanessa. She hadn't told them about Cassandra's premonition, and she was worried that they were meeting Cassandra in the park.

Finally, she ran back to her room, took the gun, and slipped it into her jeans pocket, then left.

The rain had stopped, but clouds still covered the sky and reflected the city lights, giving the night a peculiar illumination. Jimena walked along the curb until she found a taxi. She took it over to Catty's house. The driver kept glancing suspiciously at her in the rearview mirror. She wondered if he saw the determination and fearlessness in her eyes. When he finally pulled the cab to the curb in front of Catty's house, he seemed relieved.

Jimena paid the driver, then hurried up the walk and rang the doorbell.

Catty opened the door, looking surprised, then quickly cautioned her to be quiet. "I thought we were meeting in the park," Catty whispered, glancing back over her shoulder as if she were afraid the doorbell might have awakened Kendra.

Jimena stepped inside. "I want you to tattoo me."

"Tattoo? I don't know how."

"You draw," Jimena explained. "That's all you need to know to do a jailhouse tattoo. I'll tell you the rest."

An hour later the tattoo of a crescent moon and star was bleeding on Jimena's arm.

"It looks good," Catty said with pride.

"Yeah." Jimena stood in front of the mirror and admired Catty's work. Excitement ran through her when she looked at herself. She glanced at Catty and knew she was feeling the same. They stared at each other's reflections.

"You look . . . like a goddess," Catty said, smiling.

Jimena remembered she no longer had her gift. Could she even call herself a goddess now? With rising self-assurance, she knew it was her rightful title. The power was inside her.

"Ready?" Jimena asked.

Catty nodded.

They tiptoed down the hallway, past Kendra sleeping in her bedroom, and out into the cloud-covered night.

CHAPTER TWENTY-FIVE

J

IMENA PACED BACK and forth in the park near the lake, holding the moon amulet in her palm, anticipating its warning. She wondered why Cassandra hadn't arrived yet. Maybe Morgan had been unable to convince her to come.

Then she caught glimpses of someone moving in the shadows, and her amulet began to pulse.

"Jimena." The word hit her as Cassandra, Karyl, and Morgan suddenly appeared, walking toward her.

A breeze flapped open Morgan's long coat. It seemed to float behind her. Karyl was dressed in his usual black, his eyes glowing and ready.

Cassandra wore her cape and impossibly high-heeled boots. Under the eerie reflection of city lights from the clouds, her pale skin and hard, black eye makeup made her look more nightmarish than pretty, but, Jimena thought, that was probably the look she wanted. When her ice-blue eyes locked onto Jimena's, a huge force pressed Jimena down. Even at this distance she could feel herself start to fall into the depths of Cassandra's endless blue eyes.

Jimena winced and pulled back.

Morgan laughed, but her laughter no longer sounded human. It was edgy and evil. She smiled derisively. "Hello, Jimena, we're here for your meeting."

Karyl's eyes widened in anticipation, then wandered slowly over Jimena's body before returning to her face.

Cassandra pushed into her mind again, and Jimena felt her will draining from her. She flinched at the feel of anger, hate, and fear that Cassandra twisted into her thoughts, but in the same moment she was overwhelmed with pity that such ugly feelings were Cassandra's constant emotions.

She knew from Cassandra's sudden grimace that she had read Jimena's thoughts and that her pity had sent Cassandra into a violent rage.

You'll suffer, Cassandra promised. The words echoed painfully around Jimena's mind.

The awful pressure remained, coming at her in waves. Jimena let Cassandra slide completely into her mind. It was the only way to distract her so that Serena would be able to sneak into Cassandra's mind, and steal Jimena's gift back. It was also the most dangerous thing Jimena could do, because Cassandra could gain complete control over her, discover the plan, and destroy Jimena. *What can harm you, can also help you.*

A current of air flowed over her. She hoped that it wasn't just the wind, but Vanessa, Catty, and Serena nearby and invisible.

From someplace deep inside her Jimena

fought to keep her plan hidden. She kept repeating the words the goddess had spoken, *"Quae tibi nocere possunt, etiam te adiuvare possunt.* What can harm you, can also help you."

"Failed goddess," Karyl smirked. "A prayer won't help you now."

Suddenly Cassandra's head wrenched backward in shock. A distressed scream came from her twisted mouth as she fled from Jimena's mind.

Jimena took three stumbling steps backward, then looked around. She hoped Serena had been successful.

Vanessa, Catty, and Serena suddenly became visible.

Morgan seemed surprised, but Karyl and Cassandra smiled.

"I told you they would come," Cassandra said smugly.

Serena quickly entered Jimena's mind and Jimena could sense her gift of premonition returning.

"Thank you," Jimena said, as the power inside her grew, feeling stronger than it ever had.

It pulsed through every cell, gathering energy. "Now let's get out of here."

"Don't you want us to stop them?" Morgan asked.

Cassandra shook her head. "No need to."

A booming noise came roaring from the earth and the ground trembled.

Jimena fell to her knees as the earth ripped open in front of her. She tried to stand again and stagger backward, but she lost her balance and sprawled inches from the edge of the bottomless abyss. The sulfurous air from the land of the dead seeped into the night air around her.

Vanessa tumbled precariously close to the edge. Catty fell next to her.

Serena keeled over the edge. Jimena leaped forward and caught her. She clasped Serena's hand and held tight.

Jimena squirmed farther over the ledge, reached down, and grabbed Serena's other hand, straining, muscles pulling tight across her back as she tried to haul Serena back.

Immediately Cassandra's words flowed into

Jimena's mind. *You wanted a meeting to talk about getting your gift back? Do you think I'm that stupid? You fell right into my plan. I knew your friends wouldn't let you come alone.*

Too late Jimena knew she had been overly eager to face Cassandra in the park. As Cassandra sensed victory, her sapphire eyes flashed with hellish triumph.

"Hang on," Jimena said to Serena. "I won't let you fall."

Morgan peeked over the edge. "You can't hold on forever," she jeered.

One of Serena's shoes slipped off and fell into darkness.

"We'll save her," Catty cried. She and Vanessa scrambled backward and latched on to Jimena.

Cassandra whooped behind them. "My premonition," she yelled with glee. "Coming true exactly as I saw it."

Jimena could feel the earth giving way beneath her.

"You've never been able to stop any of your premonitions from coming true," Vanessa said with urgency. "Is it the same for Cassandra's pre-monitions?"

"I don't know," Jimena answered helplessly, as a mound of dirt beneath her crumbled and tumbled into the pit.

Rain started to fall. Three large drops fell on Jimena's hand and rolled down to her fingers. Serena's hand started to slide away.

CHAPTER TWENTY-SIX

THE RAIN MADE IT impossible to hold on to Serena's hands. Jimena had to do something and quickly.

"I'm going to let go of your right hand," Jimena warned her, "so I can grab your left wrist. Ready?"

Serena nodded.

Jimena released Serena's right hand and grabbed her left wrist. Her hold felt firm again, but she knew it couldn't last for long. She strained and tugged hard.

At the same time Vanessa and Catty pulled her farther away from the edge.

Serena dug her toes into the sides of the cavern.

Cassandra whispered across Jimena's mind, urging her to let go of Serena's hand. Then another voice pushed Cassandra's aside and scraped around Jimena's mind, the tone taunting and so different that she turned and glanced back at Karyl.

"Don't look at him," Vanessa yelled.

Karyl walked to the edge of the chasm and looked down at her.

"Ignore him," Catty urged and tugged hard on her legs.

Listen to him, Cassandra breathed the words softly into Jimena's mind. *He has something important to tell you.*

Jimena ignored them and glanced back at Serena. "Brace your feet against the side and try to walk up."

Serena did and was able to take one faltering step.

Jimena wiggled backward.

Karyl leaned down, closer to Jimena and spoke contemptuously in her ear. "I'm the *vato*. I'm the one who came to Veto the night he got shot. I lied to him and told him you needed his help. I led him into enemy land. He thought he was going to rescue you."

Jimena could feel anger rising inside her.

"Don't listen to him," Catty said.

"They're trying to get you to attack so you'll forget about Serena," Vanessa warned.

"Like I don't know that?" Jimena yelled back at them.

Jimena strained and pulled hard. Serena took another small step, digging her toes into the fissure wall.

Large clumps of dirt fell over the side.

Jimena had to worm backward to keep from falling. Her hands were on fire but she managed to smile reassuringly to Serena. "You're almost safe now."

She yanked again and moved backward as Serena took another small step. Catty leaned forward and grabbed Serena's other hand.

More dirt and grass gave way, but this time they pulled Serena up and over the edge.

"Hurry," Vanessa warned behind them.

They fell back as the ground slumped and large pieces of earth gave way.

Karyl smiled at Jimena with his strange, hungry eyes, and Jimena knew intuitively that she didn't want to hear his next words. She turned to face him, her moon amulet casting an extraordinary white glow over his face. He didn't seem intimidated by the power building inside her.

"Cassandra gave me the power," he bragged, his eyes burning. "The power from the Inner Circle to go back in time and change one event."

Jimena stood and stepped closer to him.

"But a big one," Cassandra added with a derisive grin as she stepped next to Karyl to face Jimena.

Karyl started to speak and Jimena interrupted him, her voice low and rasping, her anger complete, "You went back in the past to lure Veto into enemy territory?"

"To his death," Karyl said.

The air trembled with Jimena's power. She pulled the small gun from her pocket and pointed the muzzle at Karyl.

Morgan screamed and took quick steps back, but Cassandra didn't flinch.

Vanessa let out a long hiss of air and grabbed Jimena's arm. "Don't, Jimena. Remember what Maggie told us. Evil only feeds evil. We never use the tools of the Atrox."

Jimena jerked her arm away and cocked the hammer on the small gun. She kept Karyl in its sights. "Maggie doesn't know anything about fighting evil."

She let an indolent smile cross her face and then spoke to Karyl. "You're not Immortal yet, are you, Karyl? Too bad. A bullet can kill a Follower, right? You ever see what a bullet does to flesh?" She could feel the jaguar awakening and padding through her veins.

But Karyl didn't seem afraid, he seemed elated. So did Cassandra.

"Stop," Serena yelled, and then she was half-running, half-limping to Jimena's side. "The

Followers grow stronger when people use violence to fight them. You're only going to put us all in jeopardy."

Karyl sneered. "Veto thought he was going to rescue you, Jimena. His concern for you killed him."

"They'll be invincible if you use the gun," Catty cried.

Jimena gripped the gun with both hands. "He can't survive a gunshot."

"You're a force of good." Vanessa tried to convince her.

"Too late." Jimena smiled and pulled at the trigger.

CHAPTER TWENTY-SEVEN

J

IMENA FIRED THE GUN into the ground beside Karyl. At the same time she concentrated and sent all her mental power twisting at him. The night filled with a strange, pure whiteness. Sparks burst into the air and continued to glow as they dropped slowly to the ground. Jimena felt lost in her power. Her nerves thrummed with excitement while her body felt exhausted from the effort.

Tiny tendrils of static electricity swept around Karyl in diminishing circles. His eyes turned blank, then dark. Without their scary luminescence, his eyes looked tortured.

Jimena pitied him now and felt sick in her heart when she considered how truly lonely and separate the life of a Follower must be. She wondered how they came to terms with the life they had chosen. Looking at Karyl now as he lay on the ground, she suspected that they never did.

"You didn't use the gun to hurt Karyl." Cassandra's words were filled with amazement and disappointment.

Jimena faced Cassandra. "Of course not, Cassandra, we don't use the tools of the Atrox. The gun was only to distract you." She threw the gun over the edge of the abyss.

Karyl whimpered with a low animal whine, then pulled himself up, and took two tottering steps backward. He stopped and looked around him as if he didn't know which way to go.

Cassandra rubbed her finger nervously over the scars on her chest.

Vanessa, Catty, and Serena lined up next to Jimena and faced Cassandra.

Morgan looked at them, then back at Cassandra and Karyl. She suddenly turned and ran.

Thunder crashed through the air.

Jimena turned quickly. The ground quaked, but this time the earth seemed to be closing.

Cassandra trembled and a low wail came from deep inside her.

"What's going on?" Serena wiped at the mud streaked across her face.

"I think Cassandra has displeased the Atrox," Vanessa said.

Cassandra cowered as if she expected a bolt of lightning or something worse to annihilate her. Her low pathetic cries were filled with fear.

"Do you think we should try to save her?" Catty's face was covered with raindrops.

"I don't think we can," Jimena mused. "She looks like she's in deep communication with the Atrox."

Cassandra let out a cry, then turned and slowly walked away.

The ground shook and roared with thunder. The earth closed completely and Jimena knew they had won for tonight.

CHAPTER TWENTY-EIGHT

AFTER SCHOOL ON Monday the girls met at Pink's. Jimena was late because she had stopped at church to keep her promise to the goddess. Her grandmother was proud of the way she now prayed daily for the souls lost in purgatory. Jimena liked the quiet and dark and peace inside the church. She had told her grandmother about her promise to the goddess. She didn't tell her everything about that night, but her grandmother had smiled and said she suspected that God had many good spirits to help keep watch over the people of earth.

Jimena bought three chili dogs and joined her friends, who were already sitting around a table in the back. They didn't look like they were enjoying the late afternoon sun or their dogs.

Jimena sat down. "So what's up?"

Serena was the first to break the silence that held the table. "Stanton's disappeared."

Vanessa lifted her sunglasses, then looked around to make sure no one was listening. "The Atrox probably sent Regulators after him."

"Are you sure he's disappeared?" Catty took a bite of hot dog and spoke with her mouth full. "I mean, how would you know if he disappeared or was just doing what Followers do."

"Trust me," Serena answered with a glare. "I know. Something's wrong. It's like he's vanished. I'm going to go looking for him again."

"You have to be careful," Vanessa warned.

"Let's talk about something else." Serena tried to act as if she wasn't bothered, but she kept raking her fingers through her hair and glancing at her watch.

"What time is it?" Catty asked finally.

"Almost four." Serena took in a deep breath. "I gotta go."

"Do you want me to go with you?" Jimena asked.

Serena shook her head. "No. This is something I need to do alone."

Vanessa shrugged, but Jimena could tell she was unhappy with Serena's decision.

Serena started to leave.

"Remember we're here for you if you need us," Vanessa said.

"Yeah, don't think you have to be like me," Jimena added. "And do it on your own."

"Wait." Catty stood. "I have to leave, too."

"Where are you going?" Jimena asked with a sly smile.

Catty seemed to blush. Maybe it was just the heat of the sun. "I got a study date with Chris."

"Study?" Vanessa's smile was huge. "Since when do you study?"

"And on a date," Jimena teased. "You must like Chris a lot."

"I like him." Catty smiled contentedly.

"Let's go," Serena added impatiently.

"Jimena, do you want to come with me to my ballroom-dancing class?" Vanessa offered. "It'll be fun."

"No." Jimena smiled back at her. "Go on," she insisted. "I need time to think, anyway."

"You sure?" Vanessa asked.

Jimena nodded. She waited until Vanessa had left with the others, then she got up and strolled through the alley behind Pink's and started walking down Melrose. She hadn't gone far when a horn honked. She turned. Collin's utility van pulled up to the curb.

"Hey," he shouted. "You need a ride?"

She shifted her head to the side. "Are you making a career out of following me around?"

"Maybe," he answered.

She glanced at him and wondered why she felt so happy to see him.

"You want to go down to the beach?"

She shook her head, but then she looked into his clear blue eyes and the wrong word came from her mouth. "Okay."

"Great." He jumped from the van, came around to the passenger's side and opened the door.

She hesitated. Why had she said okay? She didn't want another relationship. It would hurt too much when it was over. Besides, a dull ache for Veto still filled her heart.

"Maybe I shouldn't," she said, but even as she spoke the words her feet betrayed her and she walked toward the van.

They parked the van, then walked down Colorado Avenue and onto the Santa Monica pier. Twice Collin tried to hold her hand, but she pretended she had an itch on the side of her face that needed to be scratched.

"Let's walk along the shore," he suggested.

They took off their shoes and walked in the sand at the water's edge.

Collin looked out at the water. "I'm glad you and Serena finally told me the truth."

"Yeah?" A breeze ruffled through her hair.

Collin took her hand. She hadn't anticipated his touch and a sweet excitement rushed through her.

"It explains a lot." He smiled, then he looked at her oddly.

"What?" she asked.

His arm slipped around her. "I've never kissed a goddess before."

She pulled away from him and stepped quickly down the beach.

A sudden gust pushed against her. She stopped. The wind swirled, making her clothes flap around her, and in the circling wind she thought she heard Veto telling her to go back to Collin. *He'll treat you fine.* The wind died to a caress of air across her cheek. Then it was gone.

Collin walked up to her. "Do you want me to take you home?"

She shook her head and rested her hands on his chest. "Not yet," she answered.

He didn't move to kiss her but stared at her, unsure.

Her anticipation made her desire grow and when his warm lips finally touched hers, her body filled with happiness. He kissed her long and slow, the way he had in the premonition. And as the kiss continued, warm and intoxicating, a stream of swiftly moving pictures filled her mind, all showing her with Collin. She smiled to herself, knowing that her premonitions always came true.

Don't miss the next

DAUGHTERS OF THE MOON book,

The secret scroll

A LONG HISS OF AIR escaped Catty's lungs. She stood motionless, waiting for the person to speak. When they didn't, she rushed to give an explanation. "I'm sorry," she said, assuming it had to be a security guard. "I took the elevator, then the lights went out and I got lost."

The person didn't answer. Their silence baffled her.

She tried to turn her head to see who stood behind her but when she did, a gloved hand gently stopped her.

"What?" Catty whispered nervously.

"Don't turn," the person said softly. The

voice was magnetic, young sounding, and definitely a guy. It also seemed familiar.

"Who are you?" she asked, still trying to identify the voice.

Then he spoke her name quietly. "Catty."

A shock ran through her. "How do you know my name? Do I know you?"

"I have something for you," he said, ignoring her questions.

There was a rustling behind her and then the gloved hand reached over her shoulder and gave her something that looked like a thick piece of paper.

She took it and recognized the feel of parchment. She held it close to her eyes. It was a lavishly decorated manuscript. The gold first letters caught the light from the hallway and sparkled. Strange birds and exotic animals hidden in a tangle of foliage and fairy-tale landscapes lined the borders.

"You're giving this to me?" Catty asked. "Is it stolen?"

"It belongs to you."

"Me?" She smoothed her hand over the swirling script.

"Take the manuscript and use it," he instructed.

"Use it how?"

"The manuscript contains the answers to your questions."

She wondered who he was. She wanted to turn and see his face but every time she tried, his hand held her cheek firmly.

"I don't understand," she murmured at last. "What questions should I have?"

He paused for a long moment. "Read the manuscript. Then you will know."

Discover the secrets of the
DAUGHTERS OF THE MOON

DAUGHTERS OF THE MOON # 1
GODDESS OF THE NIGHT
0-7868-0653-2

DAUGHTERS OF THE MOON # 2
INTO THE COLD FIRE
0-7868-0654-0

DAUGHTERS OF THE MOON # 3
NIGHT SHADE
0-7868-0708-3

DAUGHTERS OF THE MOON # 4
THE SECRET SCROLL
0-7868-0709-1

**LOOK FOR BOOK #5: THE SACRIFICE AND BOOK #6: THE LOST ONE
IN SEPTEMBER 2001**

LYNNE EWING is a screenwriter who also counsels troubled teens. In addition to writing all of the books in the Daughters of the Moon series, she is the author of two ALA Quick Picks: *Drive-By* and *Party Girl*. Ms. Ewing lives in Los Angeles, California.